Words On A Wall

Ian Sharman

A collection of flash fiction and poetry originally written for the Elephant Words website between December 2008 and August 2015.

Elephant Words (est. 2007) is all about seeing how different writers respond to the same image. Every Sunday a new image is posted, and during the week new short writing is posted inspired by that image. The writing can be any format or genre, limited only by imagination!

www.elephantwords.co.uk

ISBN 978-1-911243-20-5

Book design by: Ian Sharman

www.markosia.com

Second Edition

Confession

DEC 03, 2008

At night they come to life…

They crawl down the tower, cloaked in the shadow of darkness, keeping to the edges of perception like some long forgotten evil at the corners of your mind. They seek me out, I hear them scratching at the door, and before I know it they're here, inside my head. They claw their way inside and burrow deep inside my darkest secrets. They reach within my soul and find the inky blackness that I hide from everyone. They bring it all to the surface and make me do things. Things that I would never do. Except, in my heart, I've done them a thousand times.

Oh, the deeds they make me do… The blood, the violence, the violation. I beg my memory to forget, but it's all so clear to me, laid out before my recollections in a perfect vision of ecstatic depravation.

Each night I wash the blood from my hands, but as I wake it still remains. I am stained, wholly and utterly, and no amount of water can ever cleanse my soul.

The uniformed man leans over the table that separates us. I can see the horror and the disbelief in his eyes.

"One more time, for the tape, tell us what happened on the evening of the fourth…"

I've lost count of the times I've told him now… I know I have no real defence… And so I begin again…

"At night they come to life…"

It's cold in here...

DEC 15, 2008

Damn it's cold in here...

They said I wouldn't feel anything. That it would be just like going to sleep, and that I'd wake up years from now, when they'd discovered a way to reverse the debilitating condition that's wasting all of my muscles, including my heart, and it would feel like no time has passed.

I suppose there was no way they could know, really. It's not like anyone has ever gone through this process and then been woken up before. It's funny, that thought never troubled me until now. Do they really know if this works or not? I was too afraid of dying to care. Which is ironic, because my wife always told me that I was too afraid to live.

She hated this idea. She said that she wouldn't be able to properly mourn me and move on if she knew I was technically still alive somewhere, "frozen in a block of ice." She said that I was selfish to do this, and I suppose she was right. My children thought it was cool (no pun intended) that daddy was going to be "an ice man" and see the future.

Good Lord I'm bored. I could be stuck like this for hundreds of years. I hope they've found a cure for insanity by the time I'm thawed out, as I'm likely to need it. I wonder what the future will be like? Will we have flying cars, teleporters, personal jet packs? You know...I'm sure we were supposed to have those by the year 2000, it feels like all my comics lied to me. Hopefully we'll have world peace, and robots will do all the work so we won't need money, and we can have endless days filled with leisure and pleasure. Mind you, they've been predicting that since the sixties...another thing that science fiction got wrong.

I hope they still have steak when they thaw me out. That's the first thing I'm going to do...have a nice steak....

...

Outside the cryogenics facility a middle aged man in a grubby orange overall loads a canister of gas covered in warning labels into a beaten up white van, while a man in a crumbled suit, carrying a clip board looks on.

"Is this the last of them, guv'?" asks the man in the overalls.

"Yeah, once you've got that on board we can move on to shutting down the machinery inside," replies the man with the clip board.

"Seems a damn shame to me, these folks are expectin' to be woken up and cured," says the man in the overalls, safely stowing the last of the gas canisters on his van.

"It would seem that demand for cryogenic freezing has fallen off rather sharply since the economic downturn, this company simply stopped paying its bills, which was when we were called in," replies the suited man, rather matter of factly.

"Damn shame, if you ask me….damn shame…"

…

…it's cold in here…

Four Words

DEC 27, 2008

The boy ran through the park, his companion, Mr Balloon at his side. For the briefest moment it was just the two of them, the rest of the world melted away and he was lost in a place where a boy and his balloon could go anywhere and do anything. That was rudely shattered as he remembered that his brother was chasing him around the tree, and so suddenly it was just the two of them, their balloons and the tree…and they were happy.

They'd spent a brilliant day in the warm sunshine playing by the river. Mummy and Daddy were there, so was Nanny, and his uncle and aunt and their new baby daughter, his *cousin*…a new word for him. He felt so safe and secure having his whole family around him. Everything was as it ever had been and ever would be.

His brother, if truth be told, knew differently. He felt a little less secure, he knew that things weren't as they ever had been. They didn't, for example, go to that church anymore, Daddy had a new job, they lived in a new house and, well, he was sure he remembered a time when Daddy didn't sleep on the sofa.

They both ran off across the park, barely glancing back at their parents. After all, they would always be there, looking out for them, that was the one thing that would never change. That was the one thing they could always be sure of.

Later, some other place, but by the same river. The two boys weren't there, they were at home, tucked up in their beds, little knowing that four words were about to change everything. It's strange, it should take more than four words, really. It should take hours of debate, it should take careful consideration, a weighing up of all the facts. But no, it just takes four words.

Mummy and daddy stood outside the cinema, a cool breeze blowing at them across the river. "Are you ok?" she asked him, the same thing she'd asked him a thousand times before. However, this time, for some reason, he'd decided not to lie and say, "I'm fine."

Instead those four words came out that would change the lives of those two boys forever. Four simple words that could never be unspoken. For once he spoke the truth, and everything changed.

He simply said, "I'm just not happy."

How the War Beg
Began

JAN 02, 2009

Ladies and gentlemen, before I announce the findings of our recent scientific inquiries, I believe it would be rather remiss of me not to place them in a proper historical context.

For many thousands of years there has been one source of disagreement and conflict which has vexed mankind like no other. One simple area of the human experience which has given rise to more disputes and acrimony than any other topic, and that, my dear friends, is quite simply – religion!

From the earliest times man has argued over whose God is greater; whose God is real and, even more fundamentally, whether there is any God at all. Christians have fought with Muslims, Muslims have fought with Hindus, and pretty much everyone has fought with the Jews. Even those who don't believe there is a God have joined the fray, as on many occasions we've seen the forces of secular, atheist governments take arms against the forces of religion.

The only reasonable response to this is to seek quantifiable scientific proof. Is there a God? The only way to be sure would be to die; as that's the one time I think we can all agree that we will finally meet our maker. And so I, with the help of my learned colleagues, have taken it upon myself to explore this undiscovered country which we call death. I, ladies and gentlemen, have been to the other side, and I am now in a position to finally reveal to you… the truth.

The truth, my very good friends, is that despite the very extensive earthly success of the major religions, it turns out that the Poga Poga tribe of the Amazon basin were right all along. God is a tiny terrapin who wants nothing more than to be gently held.

And so, people of Earth, before we move on in a new era of peace and understanding, in which we can do little more than celebrate the universal brotherhood of man, it simply remains for me to ask if there are any questions you have for me?

Yes… yes, I see… the gentleman two rows back… with the blue jacket and your hand in the air, what would you ask of me?

"I was just… well… just wondering… um… exactly *how* would he like to be gently held?"

The Dragon's Heart

JAN 14, 2009

He'd stood watch over the tomb for a thousand years. Quietly waiting for the visitors to come. For the thieves and vagabonds in search of the untold wealth that lay within. Precious gems, hoarded by the kings of a Persian empire, gold and silver from the ancient continent of Mu, and the combined wisdom of generations of Chinese wizards and philosophers.

He'd seen so many come over the years, from the very day that his master's lifeless body was first interred within those cold, stone walls. None ever left. The traps within had been so artfully conceived, so fiendishly devised, that not one of the hapless criminals had ever managed to circumvent those cruel devices. Their broken and battered corpses littered the halls and passageways, a mute warning to those who would foolishly consider themselves worthy of the bounty that lay within.

The petty criminals had, eventually, been superseded by the archaeologists. Those learned men with their books and their scientific instruments. They had considered themselves superior to the simple robbers and brigands who had come before them, but they were no different. Their blood flowed red just the same, and stained the walls of the cold, dark tomb in the same random, crimson patterns as the thieves' had done. The lure of ancient wisdom and wealth beyond imagining kept them coming though, and the endless string of mysterious disappearances seemed to do naught but encourage their curious minds.

Then she had come, the beautiful Englishwoman, with her hair tied back in a neat pony tail, a look of determination etched on her face. Her eyes betrayed a depth of experience that her lithe, youthful body denied. As he watched her enter the dark, forbidding portal beneath him, a shiver of anticipation ran through his cold, scaly body. This one would be different. At last.

He'd not been wrong. He'd waited, patiently, as the hours passed, and though no-one had ever returned from that place before, somehow he knew. He was not to be disappointed. The woman fled from a cloud of dust issuing forth from the ancient gateway beneath him. She stood, triumphant, holding not some great and valuable gemstone, or some ancient scroll of aged wisdom. No, she had, of all the treasures sealed within, found perhaps the most precious item of all. A tiny fragment of a lost empire that had once spread across this world, and beyond. Still, after more than a thousand years, beating slowly, steadily…a dragon's heart.

He readied himself. This was the task that he had been created to fulfill. The treasures of this ancient tomb were his master's, and his master's alone, they must never be allowed to leave this place. With a low, guttural growl, he bared his fangs and leaped from his hiding place.

The beautiful Englishwoman turned and drew her guns…

My Guitar Lies Bleeding In My Arms

JAN 20, 2009

The music bled out of her, hot chords splashing to the cold, hardwood floor. An incendiary torrent of bloody riffs and licks spilling from the open gashes at her wrists. I let the crimson tide of inspiration wash over me, a baptism in pain and suffering that would inspire a million songs of teenage heartache and depression. The muse would visit me like this in my darkest moments, promising me everything; her supple, dead body speaking of pleasures never fulfilled, but ultimately all she delivered was emptiness.

She was so young, she should have been full of life, but the pale skin stretched too tight over sharp bones and the deep, dark ringed, sullen eyes spoke of her pathetic, wasted existence. She made me sing of lost and unrequited love, as my guitar gently wept for her. My heart would break, filled with grief and remorse, every night that I lay with her wicked six-stringed beauty.

She was a cold, unforgiving lover, who would whisper dreams of glory in my ears, and then leave me with my sad and empty life of abject anonymity. Her love blinded me and cut me deeply to the core, with its teenage fears of loss of innocence and the dark desires of approaching adulthood.

I looked down at my blood stained white guitar but she was all that I could see, sharp, minor.

The New World

FEB 07, 2009

He was in the airport in Baltimore when he realised he'd been travelling for a full twenty four hours. He recalled sitting, hunched over his PC at home in England and thinking he'd got a great deal, flying via Iceland instead of direct. It had saved him a couple of hundred pounds, but added about nine hours to his journey. Still, it was an adventure, and that's what this trip was all about.

The other people on the second leg of the journey, from Iceland to Baltimore, had all seemed rather absorbed in themselves as they flew over Greenland. He couldn't tear himself away from the window. It had taken him a while to realise what he was looking at. A mighty expanse of ice filling the horizon, eventually meeting the sea in a giant glacier flowing through a mountain pass. As glacier met ocean it broke into a thousand tiny chunks of ice. Except, they probably weren't tiny… That's why it had taken so long for his mind to fully comprehend what his eyes were seeing…his sense of scale had been completely messed up.

He'd travelled before, sure, and had crossed Europe in a minibus to visit the refugee camps in Macedonia during the Balkan war, but this was different. Up there in the sky, seeing the ice stretch away for miles into the distance, until it was impossible to tell where the ice ended and the sky began, he suddenly realised just how big the planet was. It seems trite, almost a cliché, but the world had seemed so small before. He spent his time working with and talking to people from across the globe. The internet had brought the world to his doorstep. But now he realised that the world wasn't a smaller place at all, it was vast.

For some reason he always picked the wrong queue in airports, but he didn't mind. He'd been travelling for a full day, and the extra time spent waiting in line to get through immigration really didn't matter to him. The people shuffled forwards and he watched them, everyone feeling nervous, everyone feeling guilty, whether they had something to hide or not. He reflected on the flight, the sights he'd seen, the new breadth his mind had acquired and wondered if anyone else waiting with him had felt the same. Maybe they did, or maybe they'd been too busy eating peanuts, or reading a book, to stop and look out of their window. Finally the lines dwindled and it was his turn to approach the desk. His fingerprint was scanned and his picture taken, like something out of a sci-fi movie, and the large, intimidating man asked him what had brought him across the Atlantic Ocean. Like so many others the official's demeanor changed at the mention of comic books, and despite the oppressive security measures he felt welcomed into this new country.

He had been travelling for twenty four hours and yet an evening at a bar, and time spent with new friends, lay between him and sleep. He didn't care, he'd set out from home looking for a new life, and here, in a new world, the adventure had only just begun.

With A Silent Scream

FEB 25, 2009

Trapped in a box with a silent scream.
Outside the city beckons but he dare not leave.
Inside his heart bleeds.
Three words said had drawn him here,
So easily spoken but not meant.
A promise made in words,
And broken in deeds.

Trapped in a box with a silent scream,
And yet inside he still longed to believe,
That all she'd said was true and real.
Like a fool he waited,
And clung to hope.
The tears came easily now,
He saw no reason to fight them.

Trapped in a box with a silent scream,
Yet still he waited for her return,
As the bitter taste of betrayal,
Rose in his throat.
Those three words repeated,
And foolishly still believed,
He did not leave.

Trapped in a box with a silent scream,
And still the taste of her lips lingered,
The sound of her voice filled his ears,
Blinding him to the truth,
That she wasn't coming back,
And it was time to leave,
Alone.

Every Cloud

MAR 03, 2009

Yes…yes, officer, I have been drinking…

It's my mate's birthday. Well, I say my "mate", he's just a guy from work really, we get on okay, but I guess I probably wouldn't normally choose to socialise with him. But, you know how it is when it's someone's birthday and everyone's going down to the pub after work, it just seems rude not to. I was only going to have a half, really, but he bought me a pint, and so did Mickey, and then it was my round so, well, I didn't think it would do any real harm, would it?

They're good lads, really, and I didn't want to spoil their fun by being the boring one sitting in the corner with a glass of Coke. I suppose I'll lose my license now, but, well, it's not the end of the world, is it? The bus to work goes straight past my house, I guess I'll just have to get used to getting up a bit earlier in the morning. Besides, I need to lose a few pounds and all the extra walking I'll be doing will do me good. Every cloud has a silver lining, eh?

I know, it was stupid of me to drive, but, it's only ten minutes in the car to get home, I really didn't think it would do any harm. I guess not thinking was the problem. I…I really don't know how it happened. One minute I was driving along… and…well, I was concentrating so hard on driving, it seemed to take so much effort just to do the simple things…the next thing I knew I'd gone into the side of that car.

Oh, damn, the people in the other car, are they…?

Oh, thank God for that, I can't believe I didn't think about that earlier.

What…?

What little boy on a bike?

I didn't see a little boy on a bike…

Little Girl

APR 02, 2009

They'd left Liverpool full of hope. The journey across the Atlantic had been somewhat traumatic, mostly spent below decks while his wife was violently sick. The sea, it would seem, did not agree with her, or, rather, she did not agree with it. The child, his precious little princess, had been small then, and oblivious to the depravations of a third class Atlantic crossing. They were packed like meat into large, communal, windowless cabins, with nothing but the lurching of the ship through the waves to let them know that they continued to make progress across the vast, briny wastes. Only the hope of a new life in a new world kept their spirits up.

And what a new world it was that greeted them. At first his heart filled with despair upon arriving in New York. Grimy, dirty and filled with the Irish, he wondered if they wouldn't have been better off back home. But no, he'd come here in search of the one thing he knew he could never find at home, freedom for him and his kin. With the last of their money he bought them a small wagon, loaded it with provisions and headed west. West to a new life, a life full of hope and happiness. A life where he would be free to be the master of his own destiny. His wife was just pleased to be off the ship, and while the wagon was small, she was happy to call it home for a while.

The child seemed exhilarated by the wide open spaces which they travelled through. He looked at her and saw his future, this land was theirs and she would claim it all.

That hope now seemed like such a distant memory. The vastness of this land had turned from a thing of wonder, a bountiful opportunity to be seized upon, into a terrible curse. The hills rolled by one after another, never ending it seemed…and the horizon always stayed so far from their reach. They'd packed enough food for a month, but they'd been travelling for three. He was no hunter, he hadn't even thought to buy a gun, and there's only so much grass you can eat before your belly rebels.

The girl sat upon his knee, the sweet, round, plump, healthy child. She smiled at him, little understanding the solemn, harsh expression he and her mother both wore. They would eat well tonight, at least, and they could always have another child.

Broken Wings

APR 08, 2009

Awake…again.

Sober…again.

I slowly sit up, the sunlight fighting a war against my mind. For some reason my eyelids seem ineffective against its vicious invasion. With the morning's bitter attack of sobriety comes the realisation that the pain that is usually so effectively masked by vodka is now being fully felt. I reach for the bottle on the windowsill, knocking over one of the little Russian dolls as I do so. I wonder, for a moment, if there's someone inside of me…and then I remember. My stomach convulses and my mouth is full of vomit, which I quickly swallow. I follow it with a mouth full of clear, hot liquid from the bottle, hoping that as it slides down my throat it will take the pain with it.

I lost something, years ago, I don't remember what it was now. I just know I've been looking for it. It feels like forever.

I drag myself out of bed, bottle in my hand, and make my way downstairs. I sit, slumped in my worn, old arm chair, the sun cruelly striking me through the window. I take another hit of vodka, and another, but the pain's still there, damn it. This worked yesterday, and the day before that, and…I can't remember how many days it's been now. Is it weeks? Months? Years? I look at the bottle and wonder how much of my life it's taken.

I remember now, that thing I lost, it was the other half of my heart. Strange thing is, I don't seem to remember ever having it. I thought I'd found it a few times, but I was wrong. So very wrong.

The clear liquid in the bottle runs dry as I pour the last drops into my mouth. I shake the bottle, hoping that those last few precious drips will be the ones to take the pain away. I am wrong, they do no such thing. The tears begin then, slowly at first, a small river of hurt down my face. They're followed by sobs as I drop to my knees. In the distance, far away, I hear someone screaming, it's several minutes before I realise it's me. The pain turns to rage, the bottle flies from my hand and shatters into a million pieces against the wall.

I'm on my knees. The storm inside has passed and all I'm left with is silence. Inside I feel numb, empty. I'd covered the pain for so long, and now, having let myself feel it, was it gone? No…it was still there, but its grip on me had loosened.

I'm staring at the floor, I don't know how long for, when I see it. A small piece of my heart, just sitting there. A tiny shard of heart on the floor. It looks so small and fragile, I wonder where the rest is, and for a moment despair of ever being able to put it back together. Then I see another, and another, a trail leading towards the front door. I follow them and they lead me outside onto the road. The road looks different today. Today the road is paved with broken dreams and shattered illusions, and the shards of my broken heart lead me along it.

At the end of the road, far in the distance, I see a girl. She is radiant, like the sun, but her light doesn't wound me. It's warm, and comforting, and it draws me closer to her. Her beauty blinds me to it at first, but then I see that stretched behind her is a trail of broken pieces of heart, just like mine. In her hands she holds a box, and she offers it to me. I take it, almost afraid to look inside, afraid of what I might find. I needn't have been afraid, for finally I've found it, the other half of my heart.

I remember something, something I've had for as long as I can remember. I've carried it with me wherever I go. Through the good times and the bad times it's always been there, but until now I never knew what it was. I reach into my pocket and pull out a small package. Wrapped in velvet to keep it safe, the most precious thing to me, it's the other half of her heart.

Into The Light

APR 20, 2009

He watched her walk back into the light, as always his heart broke a little, wondering if this would be the last time he'd watch her leave.

They'd met here, in this place between the light and darkness, every year for a thousand years. He still remembered the time they'd first met. It had been here, or somewhere very much like it, they'd both been sent to observe some significant event in human history, the city had been changing hands once again. Observe, but don't interfere, that was always the instruction. So they'd waited, and with nothing to do but talk, the unlikeliest of friendships began. He couldn't deny that she was beautiful, as were all of her kind, but there was something more that had drawn him to her, something deeper within that spoke to some rebellious feeling inside his heart.

He'd returned a year later, he was never sure why, and yet he found her there, waiting for him. So they talked, as they talked every time they met. They shared a love of art, and a fascination with the fact that a race so predisposed to destruction and savagery could have the capacity to create works of such transcendent beauty. They rarely talked about the war, about the things that separated them, except for a short exchange, which was almost word for word the same every year.

"We've both read the book, you know, we know how it ends," she would smile and say to him.

"The ravings of a mad man," he would laugh. "We both know they'll never be ready for the return, if he came back now they'd just kill him again, and his so-called followers would be the first in line to string him up."

She would always agree, and the conversation would naturally turn to something else. They never seemed to run out of things to talk about and, after a millennium, he supposed they never would. She was so easy to talk to, so easy to be with, and that just made the fact that they could never really be together that much harder to bear. However, the thought of an endless existence without these little moments with her was unbearable, and he could see in her eyes that she felt so too.

The time always passed so quickly between them. They both knew that if they spent too long together they'd be missed, and questions would be asked. As much as they wanted….no…not wanted…needed to be together, he couldn't live in her world, nor could she live in his.

He watched her walk back into the light, his lips still burning from his angel's kiss.

In My Head

MAY 08, 2009

I lie in the bath and hold the razor blade in my head. Everything surrounds me, encases me. Trapped again, no escape, no way out, all is darkness, lies, deceit. All is lost, the future, certainty. All came crashing down around my ears. No, I brought it down, brought it all upon myself. And so I lie in the bath and hold the razor blade in my head.

I see my father coming home, wondering where I am, not bothered too much, I've probably just gone out, maybe for another one of my walks, I'll probably be back soon. It's never long before he needs the toilet, though, and so he finds me. It takes him a moment to realise that it's not just red water. I wonder, does he cry? Does he fall to his knees in despair at the loss of his son? Or does he just take it in his stride like everything else. Just another one of my messes to clear up. I can only remember seeing him cry once. Seriously cry. Weep is probably the right word. We were watching Schindler's List.

I lie in the bath and hold the razor blade in my head. I'm not sure I want to know the answer to those questions. I'm not sure if I'd have to watch and find out.

I see my children hearing the news for the first time. I watch my eldest son's heart break again. Just like it did when he properly realised that mummy and daddy didn't love each other anymore. I watch him die that little bit more inside, and blame himself, just like he always does. Christ, he's only seven, how can he think he's a bad person already? I watch my youngest shrug it off and know it's not going to hit him for days, months, maybe years. I hear him ask his mother when he's going to get to see daddy again, and I see her heart break as she has to explain it to him again, and again, and again.

I lie in the bath and hold the razor blade in my head. How can I even think these things?

I see my mother and my sisters, and wonder if they saw it coming all along or if they thought it would never come to this. I bet they all thought I was stronger. I hate to disappoint them. You'd think I'd be used to it by now. They all wanted me to be different things, and I couldn't be any of them. I couldn't be anything.

I lie in the bath and hold the razor blade in my head. A way out? I'm sinking fast, if only someone would fine me here. If only someone would find me. Someone.

I see her in the clouds, an angel, a dream, my saving grace.

I see her in the clouds. I don't know how she found me here. I don't know who sent her.

A hand holds mine and pulls me out. I drop the razor blade and don't look back.

Now I lie in the bath and hold her in my head.

Watch It Go

MAY 14, 2009

At first it had been a blessing, or, at least, that's what she'd been told. Everyone was so happy, she couldn't help but feel happy too. Everyone promised to help when it came, but that's what people do. You think they mean it at the time because you don't know any better, but it's only once you're alone with the child that you find that they're nothing but empty promises.

Her anticipation had grown as it had grown inside her. She imagined holding the darling thing in her arms and loving it as it loved her back. The reality had been something different. Nights and days filled with screaming and crying and needing. Of course, it was always wonderfully behaved when anyone else came to visit, so she felt like a madwoman telling them how hellish it really was. So she kept it to herself, buried it deep down inside, and tried to block out the child's screaming.

People told her it was normal to feel detached at first, that bonding came in time, but time came and went and she felt no closer to it. She didn't know how to be a mother. What was motherhood to her? Beating, bitching, criticising…that was the example she had to follow. Crippled by the fear of unleashing her emotions upon it, instead she locked them all inside, and remained cold, aloof.

Something had to give eventually and so one day she put the child in her car and told it that they were going on an adventure. They drove all day, and, mercifully, as always, the motion of the car lulled it to sleep. They reached the coast as the sun began to touch the horizon, transforming the sea into a radiant golden carpet. She would have been moved if she'd felt anything at all.

It always liked splashing in water, and so she took it down to the shore and told it that a special treat was waiting for it in the water. She knew the coast dropped off sharply a few meters out here, and so she watched and waited as it waded out into the chilly, spring waters. There wasn't another person around for miles, while this spot was popular with tourists in the summer; it was too early in the year to attract anyone to the coast at this time of day.

The child was soon out of its depth, and the current pulled it under. She felt a release flood her entire body as it's head slipped under for the last time. She sat in her car for a good twenty minutes, half expecting it to come running up the beach towards her at any moment. Eventually she picked up her mobile phone and dialled three digits.

"Help me," she sobbed, "it's my baby, something terrible has happened…"

Future History

MAY 20, 2009

"If history has taught us anything," he mused aloud as they explored the labyrinthine corridors of the old museum, "it's that all civilisations eventually decline and fall, and their buildings and artefacts crumble and are buried within the earth for future generations to discover. Progress is not a linear process, but is cyclical. Advances are made, new technologies are discovered, but it's all eventually lost and forgotten and has to be rediscovered all over again. Recent studies of the Sphinx in Giza just highlight this. It would seem to be hugely older than was first thought and we know almost nothing about the obviously advanced civilisation that built it other than a few random clues scattered throughout our ancient myths and legends.

"I can't help but wonder what future archaeologists will think when, thousands of years from now, they start digging up the remains of our long since fallen civilisation. Thanks to the efforts of the historians, museums and archaeologists of our own age they will be completely baffled. We have systematically removed countless ancient artefacts from their proper, dateable context within the historical record and placed them in our own strata. In the future they will discover dinosaur bones buried alongside plasma screens and be forced to conclude that dinosaurs and man coexisted.

"It's always fascinated me that we see our past selves as ignorant, and interpret everything they did through the lens of superstition and religion. We arrogantly assume that we are the first people to discover science, just like every generation of teenagers assume that they're the first to discover music. Will the historians of the future treat us any better? Or will they assume that we were a primitive, superstitious lot who indulged in the worship of the strange metal boxes that they'll find in almost every dwelling? Will stories of our weird religions be filtered down to them through oral tradition as garbled tales of a war between the trickster god Mac and the all-powerful PC? What will they make of the remains of all of our cars when the engines have long since been fused into solid blocks of rusted metal, and the rubber from the tyres has perished and rotted away? All of our knowledge, all of our writing will have been utterly lost by then, they'll have no way to place anything in context, as we'll have transferred everything we know into a fundamentally impermanent digital format. The internet will have quite literally disappeared without a trace.

"So you see, our constant quest for progress has robbed our future selves of any meaningful history of our own race…and that's what I'm going to write about this week."

"Oh, Ian…" she sighed, a sweet smile playing across her lips as her beautiful, grey eyes filled with a loving pity, "once again you've shown a fundamental misunderstanding of what a story actually is…"

Half Remembered Tale

JUN 01, 2009

Yeah, so there's this tricycle, and it's in a car park, and… um…stuff happens, and it's great. No, really it is.

There's this twist at the end, see, and everybody laughs.

That's the problem with jokes, I always remember the punch line and then have to work back from there to figure out what the joke is. Like, there's this one that ends "Now Hans that do dishes is a soft as Jervais, with mild, green, hairy lip squid." It's a really funny joke, but I've been trying to remember how you get to the punch line for years. It just feels contrived, but I suspect that it was always contrived to begin with. Plus, you know, that's not even the Fairy Liquid slogan anymore, is it? So there's no point trying to figure that one out. I think it had something to do with a restaurant, and there's this squid…but I digress.

So, yeah, where was I? There was this tricycle…in a car park…it was a hospital car park. This kid had cycled all the way there because he wanted to be there when his girlfriend was born.

I know, that doesn't make much sense, but, you see, what had happened, is that this kid had lived his whole life before. His girlfriend had died tragically young or something and they'd only had a little time together. Then, when he died, he found himself repeating his life, but he could remember everything from the first time around. So, he decides that he's going to get as much time with her as possible this time. He remembers when and where she was born, he's a few years older than her, so he waits until the date and he goes there and meets her as soon as she's born. He's just this little kid, and she's a new born baby, but they meet and they have all this time together. She still dies young, and it's a real tragedy and everything, but at least he got to spend all that extra time with her. It's kinda' beautiful.

See, now I've forgotten what the twist was. Maybe it was all a dream or something, or they were alien robots from the planet Spaarg. I don't know.

It was really funny though, honest.

One Small Step For Man

JUN 13, 2009

Upon reflection, the easy part had been creating an engine that was capable of boosting a space craft to the speed of light. Or, at least, so close to the speed of light that it made little or no difference. Really, he had only the most basic of understandings of how they'd done it. It involved warping gravimetric fields, bending space and almost surfing along ripples in space/time. That was just physics. Nuts and bolts stuff. Sure, it was complicated, but once all the equations had been figured out, it was just a matter of building the thing. It's what mankind was good at, making things.

The hard part, he'd come to realise, was the waiting. When he'd boarded the ship, strapped himself into the flight chair, and braced himself for launch, his head had been full of the adventure and excitement of exploring new worlds. He would be the first human visitor to Epsilon Eridani, the nearest planetary system to the Earth. The newsfeeds had been full of how the breakthrough in space propulsion had made such a trip possible. How previously it would have required ark like ships, where generations would come and go during the journey, with the descendants of the original travellers being the ones who would first set foot on those distant worlds. Now, at the speed of light, this system would only take ten short years to reach. Finally, a round trip was possible within the space of one human lifetime.

Ten short years.

Ten years spent alone in a tiny capsule.

As the landing pod touched down on the first of the planet's orbiting Epsilon Eridani that he was scheduled to survey during his five year mission in the system, he hesitated a moment before flicking the "record" button on his log. This was a momentous occasion, and his words, he knew, would be beamed back to earth, travelling at the speed of light. Ten years from now, the people back home would be inspired by these words. They would be as significant as Neil Armstrong's first words from the moon.

He breathed deeply and then, with great solemnity, pressed the button and began to speak.

"Captain, captain, the trees! They speak with bees. And the dog's ears are numb. Mother says we sing at night, but we mostly sing at day."

Mostly Hopeless

JUN 19, 2009

"Here, drink your beer, you'll feel better," said Barry as he placed the full glass of beer in front of Dave.

"I've already told you I'm not drinking, water will be fine," Dave frowned.

"But I've already bought it for you, you might as well drink it," smiled Barry, pushing the drink closer to Dave.

"Look, unless the Earth is about to be destroyed to make way for a hyperspace bypass and we're going to hitch hike a ride with a Vogon constructor fleet to escape its destruction, then I'm really not interested," Dave laughed.

"Actually, there is something I need to tell you…" Barry started, a very serious look on his face.

"You're an alien, yes, I know, you told me," Dave interrupted, dismissively.

"I did?" Barry looked surprised.

"Yes, last Thursday, you were drunk, you probably don't remember," Dave replied, a little smugly.

"Well, clearly I don't remember else I would have remembered," explained Barry.

"Is this going anywhere?" Dave asked.

"Ah, yes, you see there's this Vogon…." Barry began.

"No, there isn't," Dave cut him short.

"Well, no, but there could be." Barry replied.

"No, there couldn't." Dave wasn't in the mood for this.

"But…" Barry persisted.

"No." It was a very firm "No," but Dave suspected that it wasn't going to put a stop to this.

"So, yeah, I'm totally an alien." Barry continued nevertheless.

"Really." Dave resigned himself to the course that Barry seemed determined to steer the conversation in.

"Yes, really, I'm from the planet…um…" Barry hesitated.

"You have to think about it?" Dave laughed.

"Well, it's been a while…" Barry mused.

"It's been a while since I've been to London but I don't have to think about what it's called," Dave exclaimed.

"Well, it's very hard to pronounce it using a human tongue," Barry smiled.

"Right. Drink your beer," Dave shook his head, and motioned towards the untouched pint in front of Barry.

"See, I knew you wouldn't believe me," Barry said, disappointedly.

"That's because it's not true," Dave pointed out.

"What can I do to prove it to you?" Barry asked.

"Well, you could be an alien…" Dave glibly pointed out.

"Right then, I will," said Barry as he revealed his true form.

"Oh, God, that's hideous," stated Dave, in an oddly matter of fact way.

"Only to human eyes, on my world I'm considered a real catch," Barry raised what Dave assumed to be his eyebrows as he said this.

"Really?" Dave wasn't convinced.

"No…" Barry had to concede.

"Can I get you lads anything else?" asked the barmaid as she came over to clear their glasses.

"No, that's fine, we were just leaving," Dave replied as they both stood up.

"So long," added Barry, as he slipped on his jacket, "and thanks for all the drinks."

Extras

JUL 07, 2009

He walked that way every day after school on his way home, and every day he passed the same shops and had the same thoughts.

The betting shop intrigued him and he always found himself wondering what the harm in it was. He couldn't help but think it would be worth putting a pound on a horse at 100-1. After all, if it lost, all he'd lose would be a pound, but if it won he'd be a hundred pounds better off! But then he'd see the people inside, their sad, desperate faces. No-one ever seemed happy in there. The women behind the counter looked miserable, clearly having to watch the same middle aged men squander what little money they had every day. They must have watched their hopes dashed over and over again, punctuated by the occasional win, the proceeds of which they knew would inevitable be spent the day after chasing that rush again.

Still, a pound here and there wouldn't hurt, would it? He couldn't help but think it was probably a good thing that he wasn't old enough to go in.

The shop next door fascinated him and made him nervous all at the same time. It claimed to be a sauna and offered massages. He couldn't help but feel the signs weren't telling the full story though. The blacked out windows suggested that there was *something else* going on inside, something that his underage eyes needed to be protected from. He'd heard rumours that the place was a front for organised crime, but he'd always felt that a massage parlour would be a particularly bad cover. The word "extras" would always float through his mind as he passed this place. He wasn't entirely sure what "extras" were, but he could take a good guess.

He'd never seen anyone go in there, or come out, and he imagined he'd never find out what exactly went on inside.

He thought these thoughts every day. Every day he'd pass these two shops and wonder exactly the same thing. Every day the same.

Except today…today would be different…

Today, as he passed these two shops, the same way he did every day on his way home from school, the robots attacked…

It's Not The Cough That Carries You Off

JUL 13, 2009

It started on the Saturday, he should never have gone to the pub. He knew it was a bad idea, but he didn't want to let his mates down. So despite his body aching all over, and his throat feeling like he'd been drinking razor blades, he went anyway.

He'd hoped he'd feel better once he was out, but if anything he felt worse. The evening seemed to drag on for an eternity and it was while he was in the toilet coughing up blood that he finally decided to leave.

He crawled home and disappeared under his bed clothes, hoping to feel better the next day.

Sunday came and he slept 'till noon, eventually waking to find himself feeling whole and healthy once again. He chose to celebrate with a return to the pub, a few drinks, and maybe some food would soon have him feeling one hundred percent himself again.

However, his entry to the pub was barred by several environmental health officers in white coveralls and face masks. Apparently several people had been rushed to hospital from the pub the night before, all suffering the same symptoms, and all died en route to the hospital. He shrugged and continued on to the next pub and enjoyed several pints of beer and a steak sandwich, before heading home.

On Monday morning he rose as usual and headed to the corner shop to buy his morning paper. Much to his annoyance the shop was closed and he had to walk half a mile to the next shop. The streets were oddly quiet, but he put that down to it being a Bank Holiday, and returned to his house to spend the day slumped in front of the TV. He paid little attention to the report on the local news about a recent spate of mysterious deaths, which had started at a pub late Saturday night.

Tuesday was downright odd, as there were armoured cars on the streets and soldiers in biohazard outfits telling everyone to stay indoors for their own good. It was Tuesday that he'd decided to move the TV into the cellar. He wouldn't get any reception in there, but he could hook the DVD player up to it and keep himself amused while whatever was going on outside blew over. Annoyingly the power had cut out at about ten at night. He could have sworn that he heard the sound of distant gunshots, and got the fright of his life when he heard the sound of his front door being kicked in. Whoever was upstairs hadn't bothered looking down in the cellar, thankfully.

On Wednesday morning he decided to venture out, to see if he could get a paper and find out what was going on. His front door had, indeed, been kicked off its hinges, and outside he found a burning pile of human bodies. Which, you know, was odd for a Wednesday. At the end of the street sat one of the armoured cars that he'd seen the previous day, and he could make out some soldiers in biohazard outfits slumped inside. At this point it was becoming clear to him that he was the only person left alive. At this point he realised that he really shouldn't have gone out on Saturday night.

Thursday had been a better day. He'd spotted her on his way to the supermarket to get some food. His relief at finding another human being had almost overwhelmed him and he'd swept her up in his arms and given her a huge hug. She'd helped him fill a trolley at the supermarket, and, thankfully, she'd suggested picking up some camping stoves from the camping store next door. It hadn't really occurred to him that without electricity or gas he wouldn't be able to cook the food. They'd fallen asleep huddled together in his front room under some blankets, trying to keep warm.

On Friday they had thought to turn the radio on, which handily ran on batteries, figuring that if there was anyone else out there, if it was just a local phenomenon, then the radio would let them know. There'd have to be some kind of emergency broadcast system or something. However, all they'd been able to pick up was static.

That night they'd sat together and watched the sun set over the city, both clearly lost in their private thoughts.

"Shadwell…" she began, nervously.

"Yes, Mfanwy?" he replied.

"Shadwell, it looks like we're the only people left, the last two people on earth," she said, in a small, soft voice. "Do you think it's up to us to…um…repopulate the species?"

"Look, Mfanwy," he replied, calmly but firmly, "you're a cracking girl, really you are, but you're just not my type."

How Many Beans Make Five?

JUL 25, 2009

It appeared overnight, one morning it was just there in the centre of the city, this big silver blob. Nobody thought too much about it, they assumed it was just some new public work of art. Some smiled when they saw it and went about their business, others grumbled under their breath about it being a waste of money, or about it not being in keeping with the surrounding architecture. Each department of local government assumed another had been responsible for the installation and ascribed their lack of information regarding it to typical bureaucratic incompetence.

It quickly became a popular meeting place and people could often be found sitting by it, eating their lunch, and enjoying the distorted reflection of the city's skyline in its curved sides. Nobody ever really questioned what it was and why it was there. It was just "one of those" and it was there "because".

It was some time before anybody realised that it wasn't the only one. There were four others, one in Birmingham in England, one in Lille in France, another in St. Petersburg in Russia, and one in Barcelona in Spain. Together with the one in Chicago, that made five mysterious objects, and they'd been there for months without anyone really realising. If they'd appeared in New York or Washington, London, Paris, Moscow and Madrid, then the world would have reacted far more quickly, but they didn't appear there, and so nobody noticed.

Eventually, almost a year after they'd appeared, the authorities decided that something ought to be done. It took them another six months to decide what that should be. A further six months of planning and research and they were ready to make their move, only to find a ring of protestors around the objects. People had grown used to them being there, and people don't like change. How dare the government do anything to such a beloved landmark? Besides, they'd been there for years; if they were harmful something would have happened by now.

Months passed, and court orders and injunctions were sought, and eventually the protestors were cleared.

On the day that the scientists surrounded the object in Chicago and prepared to probe it and investigate it with the instruments they'd spent months designing and building, the object suddenly rose off the ground and hovered in the air, about five feet off the ground. There was a barely audible hum and the air beneath the object shimmered like heat haze.

A booming voice resounded from the object, "How many beans make five?"

The scientists conferred and discussed, and after a few minutes one man stepped forward from the group to offer an answer. He looked back at the group nervously, receiving a flurry of encouraging nods in response, before he proffered their reply.

"Five beans make five," he declared in a clear, confident voice.

"You are incorrect," boomed the mechanical, alien voice from the object.

"We are?" replied the scientist, confused. "Then how many beans make five?"

"A bean, half a bean, two beans and a bean and a half," boomed the voice. "You were incorrect, your species is unworthy, and it will be eradicated."

Screams filled the city for the rest of the day.

Don't they always?

SEP 17, 2009

I started writing you a story,
Just the other day,
About the day I won your heart,
And it was going to say,
All the things I'd never said,
Or never said that way,
But before I finished writing it,
You took your heart away.

As they sat in the park together the sun made the highlights in her hair sparkle like a halo. His heart felt close to bursting as he held her in his arms, and she clung to him tightly as if he might disappear the moment she let him go. His hand gently caressed her perfect, soft cheek, and her soft lips met his. He looked deep into her eyes and saw his future in an instant, and there was no longer any doubt in his mind that he wanted to spend the rest of his life with this angel. And so he asked her to be his forever, and she said yes.

The rain lashed hard against his window as he awoke and the vision of perfection slipped from his mind. He had been torn from the most perfect summer's day, back to reality; it had all been a dream. No…not a dream…it had been real, even though it felt like a dream, but then she had always seemed too good to be true to him. The summer had only been a few shorts weeks ago, but the dark, oppressive sky and heavy rain clearly attested to summer's end, and the dull ache in his heart just confirmed it.

As he reached from his bed to turn off his alarm his eyes played across the collection of toys on the mantelpiece. He was in his thirties, why did he have toys? Was he so desperate to cling on to his long, forgotten youth? Perhaps it was time to grow up, and stop dreaming. Perhaps it was time to finally give up hope.

He dressed and washed and headed down to his studio to spend another day working, another day chasing a dream that no longer had any purpose. He'd given up on his dreams before; it wouldn't be so hard to give up on them again. He could go back to an empty, hollow, meaningless life again. Why not? Isn't that what everyone else did day after day after day? Living just to get drunk at the weekends, with the hope of occasional, meaningless sex with strangers to get him through the years. He felt his stomach turn, he'd never done that, and he didn't really want to start now.

In his studio he was surrounded by little fragments of their life together, every one clawing at his heart, reminding him of what he'd lost. His mind rebelled and his chest ached as he felt the tears come once again. And then he saw it.

A small package sat on his desk. Despite being marked "fragile" it looked like it had been used as a football on the post room floor. He picked it up and carefully opened it, and inside he found his bruised and battered heart. Next to it sat a note which simply read "I'm sorry, I thought I wanted this, but I don't, you can have it back."

He fell to his knees and as he did so the package slipped from his hands. His broken heart hit the floor and shattered into a million tiny pieces.

Promises broken,
Just like my heart,
Lies told,
A heart stolen,
Or given away,
I'll never be sure,
You said you loved me…

…don't they always?

River Blues

SEP 23, 2009

I'm standing on a bridge across a river.

I'm in Maidstone, outside the court house, and the river is the Medway.

I've lived near this river all of my life. It's as much a part of me as the sky, the hills around me, and the trees in the park next to my home. As I watch the water slowly slide by beneath my feet I sing to myself a song that I wrote when I was fifteen or sixteen. Back than the words just sounded good. I had no idea what love was and how it could hurt. I hadn't had my first real girlfriend, let alone been married, had kids, shared my life, my heart, with another person. I was just a kid, I knew nothing. Yet the words come back to me now and I find that for the first time I understand them all.

"Medway river blues,
Flowing by like me and yous,
One moment here the next she's gone,
Got no idea where I went wrong.
Medway river blues,
Flowing o'er my dusty shoes,
One moment here the next she goes,
Where she's at nobody knows.

But if you see her crying in the night,
Tell her not to worry I'm all right,
'Cos the future looks bright,
Yes the future looks bright on my own.
Alone, you're on your own,
And you can't keep the dreams from your mind.
Alone, you're on your own,
But you don't know what it is you have to find,
Deep in your mind,
In your mind."

As this old relic from a long forgotten me drifts through my thoughts, I look up to the grey, overcast skies. I dream of a place where the sun always shines and the cool, blue waters flow.

I think it's time to go back and start again. Time to do the things I should have done so long ago, while I'm still young. It's time to stop living with regrets and to just start living.

I can't keep wondering "what if?" anymore.

I have to know.

Through A Glass, Darkly

SEP 29, 2009

"For now we see through a glass, darkly."
1 Cor 13:12

Twelve men, good and true, sat around the table, trying to find the truth amidst a flood of clichés. There are three sides to every story, so the saying goes, yours, mine and the truth, but it was their job to find that third side amidst a muddle of exaggerations and half remembered facts. "If you subscribe to Cartesian philosophy," he joked, "then the only thing you can ever be sure of is your own existence. I might just be a figment of your imagination, so how can we ever be sure of the truth here?" They all laughed at that, but, if truth be told, it bothered him. He'd been a young man when he'd first become aware of the subjective nature of reality, that there really was no objective truth. How could there be? Two people could recount the same experience in such radically different ways, react to the exact same stimulus in fundamentally opposite terms, that it was impossible not to conclude that one's experience of reality was intrinsically bound up in one's own internal reality, and that any search for empirical, objective truth was doomed from the outset.

Even the old adage that you could, at least, trust the evidence of your own eyes was revealed to be quite clearly false to anyone suffering from the common affliction of myopia. From the age of eleven his own eyes had been telling him that the world was an indistinct, blurry mass, and it was only the glasses he'd had to wear every minute of every day since then that refined the world into the sharp, focused picture that everyone else supposedly saw. Who was to say what was real though? Who was to say that the blurred, indistinct masses he saw without his glasses weren't how the world really was? And that the in-focus world he saw through his spectacles wasn't the illusion?

Things just got more muddled as he got older. If we could barely agree on an objective definition of the nature of something so concrete as a chair, or a book, or a tree, how could we ever hope to agree on something as ephemeral as love? How do you define an emotion? How do you describe a feeling in empirical, rational, objective terms? How can you ever know that you share an emotion with someone else when you can barely explain to yourself how you feel? Let alone someone else!

So now he and these eleven other people had to figure out who was telling the truth. It sounded so simple when you said it like that. The judge made it sound so straightforward. Yet he wondered if there was really any truth to find. They bandied about words such as "innocence" and "guilt" without ever discussing the nature of an external morality, without ever contemplating its possible source. It was just assumed that certain things were inherently right and wrong. So they laughed and dismissed the question of the subjective nature of reality without a second thought, and returned to the task at hand...defining reality, and creating the future.

Defying Convention

OCT 05, 2009

Darkness, it could be said, consumes us all in the end. It creeps inevitably into our lives, slowly but surely consuming our souls. Some resist its pull, and some give in to it willingly. Some revel in the darkness, welcome it into their souls, and let it embrace them completely. For some it is a seasonal thing, as simple as the long, lingering death of summer. The inevitable departure of sunlight from the lives of many brings a gloom of the soul to accompany the grey, forbidding skies, and the long, seemingly endless, inky black nights.

These and other slightly less happy thoughts consumed his mind as he sat, brooding, behind a table full of comics that he had, over the past few years, almost literally poured blood, sweat and tears into creating. Each time a prospective customer approached his wares and dismissed them with but a cursory glance he felt a small piece of his soul die, and he struggled to suppress the tide of profanity which he felt rising within himself.

It was then that a girl came wandering up to his table. She looked awkward in a baggy t-shirt, her hair in braids. She flicked through his comics and said that they looked cool, although he could tell that she had no intention of buying them. He resigned himself to the inevitable conversation about the fact that she had no money on her. It amazed him that everyone seemed to attend these events without bringing any money whatsoever.

Instead she simply said, "Isn't this amazing?"

"Isn't what amazing?" he replied.

"This place, these people, I feel so at home," she gushed.

"Oh, yes, I guess so."

"Don't you love being surrounded by your own people?" she asked.

"My…own…people…?" he was confused.

"Yes, geeks, like us!" she replied. "It's funny how they call it a convention when there's nothing conventional about us, the normals would hate it here."

"Normals?" he wondered, aloud.

"Yes, normal people, non-geeks," she explained.

"Hmmm," he mused. "Did you like the Lord of the Rings films?"

"Oh, I loved them! Peter Jackson is a God!" she enthused.

"How about Pirates of the Caribbean?"

She giggled and mumbled something about Johnny Depp in reply.

"The Dark Knight?"

"Why so serious?" she laughed.

"Harry Potter?"

"Expelliarmus!"

"And I guess Star Wars goes without saying…even the prequels."

"Even the prequels," she nodded in agreement.

"So…what you're telling me is that you love nine out of the ten highest grossing films of all time," he said, a blank expression on his face.

"Um…" she faltered, suddenly realising for the first time that, perhaps, she wasn't talking to a kindred spirit here.

"And I'd wager that you've at least seen Titanic, too… even though you'd never admit to liking it."

His face peeled back to reveal a gaping mouth filled with razor sharp teeth and a cruel, flicking tongue which dripped with saliva. His body lurched forward and with one mighty gulp he swallowed her whole.

The folds of his face quickly slid back together and he looked around him at the array of geeks, so engrossed in their fantasy worlds that none of them had noticed him devour this young woman. He belched and smacked his lips.

"Bloody normals," he grumbled to himself. "At least they taste good."

Window To My Soul

OCT 17, 2009

My eyes, windows to my soul, what do you see in there? I can't remember the first time someone told me that they're beautiful. "Beautiful"…never handsome…that's always the word they used. From an early age I noticed a strange effect when people looked into them too long. There was a power there, and I've never been sure what to do with it. What could you see in my eyes? I wonder that sometimes. I wonder why you found it so hard to look into them. What did you see there?

Grey eyes, so cold. There was always a wall there. They may be windows to your soul, but you keep the shutters down, you don't let anyone in. I tried to see inside, but only got so far, and I think you were afraid of what you saw in mine. I wish I could look into my own eyes and see what people see. What did you see there? What was it that made you so afraid? I know you used to see yourself there…I guess that changed…

Brown eyes, so warm. So hurt. So wounded. There was a time they were all I could see, and once again I know I could lose myself in them so easily. Sometimes they sparkle with such life, and sometimes I see the pain you try so hard to hide. It's there in your eyes, so unmistakable, and all I want to do is hold you and tell you that everything's going to be all right. You're so close to me, yet so far away…and I want so much for you to just reach out and take my hand. I wonder if you ever will. We've been apart for so long, but now I know I'll always be here. If you want me, if you need me, I'll be here.

Blue eyes like fire, burning bright, drawing me in. I know I shouldn't want you but how can I resist? Blue eyes have always been my weakness. Filled with innocent desire, young passion like a drug I can never get enough of. You turn me upside down and inside out, make me crazy, make me happy, make me forget myself. I see your eyes when I close mine, in my dreams, in my fantasies. Blue eyes forever, blue eyes for never. Blue eyes are a dream. Blue eyes are a fantasy. Blue eyes are forever out of reach, out of bounds. Look but don't touch blue eyes.

My eyes closed. My eyes opened. My eyes, windows to my soul. Look into my eyes, what do you see? A reflection of you? The truth about me? Do you see my soul?

Blue eyes ringed with hazel. Power, eternity, youth and age.

Look into my eyes, what do you see?

My Friend Of Misery

NOV 04, 2009

You sit and you watch and you wait and you hope that she'll come and she'll take the pain away. You dream and you hope and you fantasise, never living, never being, never leaving the house. You cry and you scream and you protest that no one understands and never will.

And still the rain beats down on your window.

You blog about it and you tweet about it and you fill a million Facebook status updates about it. You devote a website to your pain and call it real life. You sing and you scream and you cry until you're blue in the face, until your voice is gone and all that you can utter is the strangled sound of silence.

And still the rain beats down on your window.

You sit and you wonder if this is all life has to offer and, if so, maybe you should just end it all. But you've barely begun, you've barely lived and, you know what, this isn't it, not at all. It may be a cliché but you have to know pain to truly know joy, your highs can only ever be as high as your lows are low. Who wants to live their life experiencing nothing but averages?

And still the rain beats down on your window.

So you cut and you bleed and you say it's the only way that you can cope with the pain. And all of us, those of us who've lived, we look at you with contempt, because you don't even know what pain is. You want pain? Live our lives. Live through the abuse and the betrayal and the loss that we've been through and then tell us that your pain is so bad that you have to hurt yourself. Tell us we don't understand.

And still the rain beats down on your window.

You sit and you watch and you wait and you mistakenly think this is about you.

And still the rain beats down on your window.

My Broken Life

NOV 10, 2009

The old, cracked
Broken steps
Where your head
Cracked
Broken steps
Where I watched
You
F
A
L
L
Cracked
Broken steps.

I left, your
Broken heart
Where I killed
Your
Broken heart
Where I watched
Us
B
R
E
A
K
Your
Broken Heart.

I forgot, my
Broken life
Where I left
My
Broken life
Where I watched
Me
L
O
S
E
My
Broken life.

The Room

DEC 04, 2009

"Welcome, please take a seat, we'll be with you in a moment." The serene, female voice echoed around the cold, lifeless room. Light ebbed into the room through the window, but it was winter light, stripped of all of its ability to warm him. The window added an otherworldly feel to the light, so he couldn't tell what time of day it was. It could be morning, or evening, or any other time, he didn't know. He didn't know, either, how he'd come to be there, and he wondered now where the voice had come from. There was no-one, after all, in the room, other than himself. He sat down on a single chair in the centre of the room, facing a row of empty chairs against one wall. It seemed like the right place to sit, as if the chair had been placed there just for him.

"Um…hello?" he floated the question out in the air, not sure if he really expected any response. "Can you tell me where I am? Who are you? Why am I here?"

"You are in the room," replied the voice, and he jumped a little when it spoke, "I am me and you are here because this is where you come."

"This is where I come? But I've never been here before…" he mused, although now he thought about it, the room did feel somewhat familiar.

"This is where you come to wait."

"So it's a waiting room?" he asked.

"In a way," the voice replied. "This is where you come to wait to be fixed, you were broken, again, and now you have to wait."

He felt certain that as familiar as the room felt, he'd never been there before, he would remember, and he'd remember how he got here too.

"I haven't been here before…"

"It was different then. You've been here many times before. Always a different room, but always the same place. Broken. Waiting. Alone." The voice remained calm, serene, all the time, as if explaining a simple concept to a child.

"Oh…yes…I see…" He wondered how long it would take this time. He remembered the first time he'd been here; he'd been little more than a boy at the time. It was a different room, in a different place, but it was still here. Everything was falling apart and so he'd gone there. He'd told them he was ill, but, really, he just wanted to escape. He'd sat in that room with nothing but his thoughts for company and a machine, in the corner, slowly ticking away. Then, later in life, there'd been another room, where he'd hidden away, scared, afraid, alone, wondering how he'd come to be there, wondering why. Again and again he'd come back here, to this place, shutting the world out.

He stood up.

"Please, be seated, we'll be with you in a moment," the voice stated, still as calm and serene as before.

"No."

"No?"

"Not this time." He walked over to the door, which somehow he hadn't seen until he stood up, and placed his hand on the handle.

"I really wouldn't, you've never done that before, you should just wait, everything will be okay, just give it time."

No," he said again, and as he did so he turned the handle.

Slaves Of The Cone Empire

DEC 16, 2009

They came in the dead of night, when we were all fast asleep in our beds. They came out of the mist, shrouded in vapour, silently filling the streets. Those few who saw their arrival, merely shrugged and carried on into the night. They thought nothing of these insidious invaders, so innocently emerging across the nation.

When we awoke the next day we found ourselves slaves of the cone empire. Unable to drive anywhere, hemmed in, trapped by the nefarious orange and white foot soldiers of this conical tyranny. Food supplies began to run out as people were unable to drive to out of town super markets. Starved and desperate, families began to turn on themselves, and cannibalism ran rife throughout the country. The political system collapsed and we descended into anarchy. The streets were wild, and life became nasty, brutish and short.

The cones had utterly defeated us in a single night.

Now, weeks later, as I huddle in my cold study, trying to ignore the desperate cries of the hungry and maimed who stalk the streets outside, I can't help but wonder. I wonder at how easily we were defeated. I wonder…

…I wonder why no-one thought to just move the damn cones.

The Great Crocodile

DEC 28, 2009

This is our future, this is our past, the unending circle of the ages. The mill of the gods turns slowly, and we are merely chaff to them. Just as Tereth and Akeeah were thrown to the great crocodile God, Matee, we are thrown to the wind, to be consumed by the endless passage of time.

For wasn't it as the first man, Tereth, once said, "We are but as nothing to the great Crocodile, who devours our days and consumes our nights." Did not the first woman, Akeeah, reply to him and say, "But quiet, my husband, for Matee is always but a moment behind, quietly stalking us in the darkness, hounding our days."

This is our future, this is our past, just as the shining face of the Disc looked down upon Tereth and Akeeah and their seventy two sons and frowned, does he not look down upon us too and ponder our destruction. Hide, O people, hide and cower in fear. Cover your faces in shame, for Matee returns once again to devour us.

Flee to the hills, to your roof tops, turn your tools to weapons and prepare. For Matee will turn your brothers against you, he will confuse your hearts and set them against one another. In your fear and doubt he will come and you will be consumed, the great Crocodile will swallow you whole.

Your children he will eat up and spit out, only to devour them again. So beware, O people, for like Tereth and Akeeah you will be destroyed. For you are their children, and their children's children, and the Disc has set himself against you. He sends his servant Matee to pour out his wrath against you.

O people, despair, for your end is at hand. Throw up your arms to the Disc and plead for mercy. Mercy will not come. Only Matee, only the end will come.

Goodnight Chicago

JAN 09, 2010

He stood on the bridge over the Chicago River, and looked out across the water and sighed. He was nearly back at his hotel, but he just wanted to savour the last of the night, and watch the city lights dancing across the ripples in the water. People laughed and talked in the restaurant above the marina and cars crawled by as city life went on around him, but he barely noticed any of them. Instead his mind slipped back a few hours to that moment on the train when he'd first seen her.

He was late, but he'd travelled four thousand miles to be there, so it was always going to be hard to be on time. It hadn't been until he was on the train that he'd figured out how to make his phone work in this strange, faraway land and so he'd had no way to let her know he was on his way. He spent the train ride worrying that she'd have given up and gone home after seeing the train he was supposed to be on pull up and then leave again without him stepping off. She would have had to watch the next train do the same. Now the third train was pulling in and he felt sure that she'd be worried that it would be leaving her alone on the platform again.

He stood up as the train began to slow and he strained to see through the crowd of other passengers waiting to get off. His eyes scoured the platform until he found her, one lone beautiful girl in a zebra striped dress, looking nervous and anxious.

"There she is!" he said aloud, to no-one in particular. It was just too hard to keep his excitement and relief to himself. He wished there was some way to signal to her, to let her know he was there, that she didn't need to worry anymore. It seemed as if the whole train was getting off at this station, as a huge crowd blocked his way to the exit. They all shuffled off the train so slowly as he fidgeted and fretted in his eagerness to alight from the carriage. Eventually he was free, and he ran through the crowd, knocking into an old lady on the way. He didn't realise he'd done it, not until alter when he was remembering the moment, and he felt bad for not saying sorry, but he only had one thing on his mind. He had to get to her.

She was on the opposite platform, and as the train started to pull away, he crossed the tracks behind it, running up to her. He saw the look on her face, a look of confusion and relief, as for a moment, he felt, she had no idea who this strange man in a leather jacket was, running towards her. Then before he knew it, her arms were around him and they shared their first, nervous kiss. The kiss of two strangers who knew each other better than they'd ever known someone before.

"I was afraid you weren't coming," she sobbed.

"Of course I was coming, I love you," he said, and they kissed again.

She took his hand and led him away from the station, to begin the evening they'd been dreaming of and planning for a year. Their nervousness was tangible as they walked through the hot, summer's evening air. His heavy leather jacket made him uncomfortable, and he regretted wearing it, a simple traveller's mistake, not knowing what an August night in Illinois would be like.

She led him to a restaurant, and they sat down to eat, attempting to talk. All they'd done for a year had been talk, every day, for hours, and now they were sat together and they couldn't find the words. He was worried that she was disappointed, that the dream had been better than the reality of him. He was nervous, because every time he looked at her he thought the opposite. He'd seen so many pictures of her, but nothing had prepared him for this, nothing had prepared him for being there with such a beautiful woman. All he wanted was to be alone with her, to hold her and kiss her.

They ordered their food from a waitress who seemed baffled by them. Neither of them had any appetite, they both just wanted to get away and be alone, and when they asked for the bill, their food barely touched, the waitress gave them a look of total disgust. They didn't care, they just needed to leave, to get away and be together.

They started walking, neither of them really knowing where they were going. They walked along behind the restaurant, as she tried to think of somewhere they could go and just be together.

He couldn't take it anymore. He'd come so far, and they'd spent so long apart, he just had to know if she felt the same way as him. There was only one way to find out.

"Wait…" he said, and he took her hand. She stopped and looked at him. They were standing in a wide, open alleyway; there was no-one else around. He didn't care, he didn't really notice where they were, all he could see was her, and he knew there was only one thing he could do. He took her in his arms, held her close and kissed her. She wrapped her arms around him and kissed him back, then held him tight to her, burying her face in his shoulder. They just stood like that for what felt like hours, just holding on to each other as the whole world melted away around them.

At some point the sun set, at some point the evening turned to night. He couldn't tell you when. All he could remember was the taste of her lips, the feel of her breath on his face, her touch and the way she held him as if the whole world would crumble if she let go.

The night seemed to last forever, but eventually time slipped away from them, and she led him back to the station. They curled up on a bench together, laughing and joking and taking pictures, all the nervousness of first meeting had melted away, and they were just the couple they'd always been from so far apart.

An old man waited with his son on the platform, clearly amused by the young lovers. The man heard his accent and asked him where he was from, and what had brought him so far from home. She had, of course, she had drawn him here from across the ocean and covered him with love.

He could hardly remember how he'd got back to the city. He'd drifted through the streets downtown, back to his hotel, until he reached the bridge across the river just before it. Now here he was, looking out across the water, dreaming of her, wishing she was there with him, holding his hand. Wishing he could share this moment with her, and every moment after it. He looked across the river at the city.

"Goodnight, Chicago," he smiled, "I think I'll be seeing a lot of you."

Wait... What?

JAN 15, 2010

He recklessly, foolishly hid from the light,
Cowered in fear, trembled in fright,
Hid from the rays of a bright burning Sun,
Hid from a life of laughter and fun,
Curled up in a corner full of dark and despair,
Complaining to no-one that life was unfair,
Put all of his world in a big cardboard box,
Unplugged the phone and changed all the locks,
Railed against life that had been so unkind,
Retreated for days into his own mind,
He put bars on the windows and sealed up the doors,
And pointed his finger at an invisible cause,
Of all of the misery, all of the woe,
All of the pain that his heart had to know,
And sat writing couplets that barely did rhyme,
Never realising they were a waste of his time,
For life is for living, not sitting afraid,
A cliché, I know, but the point must be made,
Unbar the windows, unlock the doors,
Stop pointing fingers, for you are the cause,
Of the rampant unhappiness that fills your life,
So end it all, quickly, I'll hand you a knife.

The Art Of Giving

JAN 21, 2010

It had started out as a single pot plant his mother had bought him to "brighten up the place a bit." He'd put it outside on the porch, thinking it stood a better chance of surviving out where nature would water it, rather than indoors where he'd forget. Visitors rarely got past the front porch, and so, he had to assume, when choosing a gift for him, they'd seen the pot plant and assumed that he liked pot plants and so bought him another one. Of course, once one pot plant had become two, it had become clear to every visitor that he had a thing for pot plants...and so they multiplied with each significant date, every birthday or anniversary, or visit from an aunt who barely knew him but felt that she really shouldn't arrive empty handed. So that single pot plant had become a collection of pot plants, and he was now "the guy with all the pot plants on his porch" and no-one ever arrived at his door without a pot plant in hand.

The porch had pretty much vanished under a sea of pot plants by this point. His utter neglect of their welfare seemed to have little or no effect on them. People said that the sea of green was "welcoming" and a "wonderful oasis of nature in the middle of the city." He found it to be a nuisance on the rare occasions that he actually ventured out of the house.

What the pot plants did do, however, was serve as a constant reminder that no-one actually knew him. Even his own mother, who had set off the whole chain of events by giving him that initial pot plant, had forgotten why she'd bought it and was now convinced that her son had a thing for pot plants. This is true of most gifts, of course. Very rarely do people actually take the time to consider what someone might actually want to be given. No, the extent of the gift giving thought process is simply "oh, they have some of these, I'm sure they'd love some more." This is how people end up with collections of thimbles, or tea spoons, or porcelain cats. This rule only fails when you actually, genuinely collect something. At this point no-one ever buys you something for your collection because "they don't know what you've got." This happens even if the gift giver lives in the same house as you, and finding out what you do and don't have would just require walking into a room in the house you share and looking. Both scenarios serve as evidence that no-one really knows you, ever. The extent of the thought behind the gift giving in each case is simply "what stuff do they have and can I get away with just buying them more of the same?"

He slumped back into the well worn, leather backed chair that sat in front of his computer. The daylight struggled in through the hastily opened curtains. Dust danced in the sunbeams and he sighed heavily. It could be worse. There was something worse than the barely thought through present.

There was the Terry's Chocolate Orange.

This is a gift which simply says "I don't know who you are and, quite frankly, I don't care." The chocolate orange is an amazing thing. When you're given one, wrapped up in shiny paper, you know instantly what it is. As you unwrap it you're already rehearsing your half hearted "Oh, thank you" and thinking to yourself "well, I haven't had one of these in a while, maybe I like them?" And you do, the first two or three segments are always quite nice, but you can't stop there and wrap it back up, oh no, you have to eat the whole thing. That's when you remember why you hate them.

He got up out of his chair, and ran his fingers through his hair. A thought had struck him. A slightly wicked thought. He walked to the kitchen, and opened the cupboard under the sink, pulling out a roll of black plastic sacks. He tore one off the roll and walked to the front door, bracing himself for the green-tinged daylight that would affront his eyes when he opened it. As he opened the door he paused for a moment, looking over the sea of pot plants. He couldn't remember who'd given him any of them; he had no idea what they even were. Some were flowers, some were ferns, that was the extent of his knowledge. One by one he picked them up and put them in the sack. It quickly filled and so he tied it up and placed it neatly by the door for the dustmen to collect, and fetched another bag. He filled that one too, then a third and a fourth, but before long his porch was clear. He smiled wryly to himself.

Now he'd find out if they actually knew him or not.

Or maybe…just maybe…he'd be getting twenty chocolate oranges next Christmas…

The Red Eye

JAN 27, 2010

He wasn't sure what was more disturbing, the lack of people or the lack of things. He'd woken that morning to find the city not only deserted, but stripped bare. Shops, houses, office blocks, they'd all been left as empty shells. Just a few scraps remained here and there. An empty shelving unit, an abandoned desk, it was more than just a ghost town, it was desolate. He would have almost welcomed the sight of a shambling zombie, or a radioactive dog, anything to shatter the oppressive silence.

It was then that he realised just how silent it was. It wasn't just the people missing, there were no animals either. There were no dogs barking in the distance, no birds singing in the trees. There was simply nothing.

Or was there?

He strained his ears and thought he could hear a faint hum in the distance. He left the empty shell of the department store he'd wandered into in the hopes that he'd be able to hear the sound more clearly.

As he emerged back into the harsh light of day, he couldn't miss the hum, and the faint sounds of things crashing in the distance, because the source of them was all too clear. In the distance, across the city, he could see a large machine, like a cylindrical tower, covered in pipes and antennae, hovering above the buildings. The air beneath it was obscured by a shimmering heat haze, and countless robot arms dangled down from it, reaching into the city, scooping things up into the behemoth's mechanical maw. A hundred smaller machines buzzed around it, flying down into the buildings below and then returning to the beast with offerings of God only knew what.

As he saw it he let out a soft gasp…and it stopped.

The machine fell silent, as did the multitude of smaller machines that surrounded it. They all stood deathly still. He held his breath as he watched a central section of the huge cylinder silently rotate.

Slowly a giant red eye swung into view and looked directly at him.

The Poets of Mars

FEB 02, 2010

The Mission Bar was one of the most notorious drinking establishments on Mars. It was also one of the oldest. Sitting in the shadow of Olympus Mons, it had been built by the first settlers, back when Mars was a staging post, the next step on from the Moon to the rest of the Solar System. In those days the pilots and crew of the star ships heading out to explore the outer planets would gather in the bar the night before their missions were due to leave and have one last drink together. Over time the facility grew, more people were needed to run it, and they had families. Service industries began to spring up around the base as pioneering business men sought to meet their needs, and in time the base became a town. That town had since become a city, and other cities had sprung up across the planet as the human race had begun to spread throughout the Solar System, just as it had spread across the Earth centuries before. Now there were colonies on every planet, from Mercury to Eris, no matter how inhospitable they seemed. If there was money to be made, resources to be mined, there were people there. Even if there was nothing of value, you could often find a small community of people who saw the remoteness as being something valuable in and of itself, often for political or religious reasons.

There was little left of that first bar, it had been extended and refurbished so many times in the years since it had been built, and few knew its heritage or the reason for its name. They just knew that it was a great place to go if you wanted to disappear into a quiet corner and slowly drink yourself into oblivion. You see, Mars, for all of its opportunity, for all of its reputation for being a gateway to the Universe, was a place that people often got stuck.

People would spend their whole lives scrimping and saving to buy a ticket to Mars. They'd tell themselves that once they got there, they'd find a job and earn the money to buy passage on a ship to one of the other planets. Some did, many never made it. All their money would go on just getting by, and the occasional night at places like the Mission Bar. They'd drink to forget the daily grind, and reminisce about the blue skies and green fields back on Earth.

The bright red neon sign outside the bar flickered as Sam walked through the door. He sat down at the bar and ordered a shot of whisky. He was young, in his early twenties, with a fresh face and a shock of blond hair on his head. He was wearing coveralls, undone to his waist, revealing a red check shirt underneath; his heavy work boots caked in red dust. His hair was matted with sweat and his face was stained with oil and grease.

"Hey, kid," the bar tender offered him a warm smile, "I ain't seen you around here, where ya' headed?"

Everyone was headed somewhere, no matter how long they'd been on Mars, no one was ever just there.

"I'm on my way to the artist's colony on Ceres," Sam replied, "I'm a poet."

"A poet, eh?" The bartender smiled. "So's Jim over there. Steve's a sculptor. An' old Herb, over there, he's writin' a novel." He indicated a succession of dishevelled, drunken men as he spoke. Sam looked them all over and his heart sank a little bit.

"What happened to them?" he asked.

The bartender looked him square in the eye, and simply said, "Mars."

She Danced

FEB 08, 2010

She danced on the beach,
In her magical shoes,
She danced on the beach,
It was quite a to-do,
Although nobody saw her,
And nobody knew,
What beat in her heart,
As she danced in those shoes.

She danced for her love,
She danced for her heart,
She danced all the day,
Until it fell dark,
Then she danced 'till her feet,
Felt incredibly sore,
So she removed those gold shoes,
And she danced some more.

The rocks did not see her,
Nor did they care,
They did not follow this girl,
With their implacable stare,
As she danced for the lover,
Who lived far away,
Across the wide ocean,
That lapped at this bay.

"Oh, come to me, love,
Come to my side,
Fly here, or sail here,
I don't care how you ride,
I'll dance for you, lover,
In my golden shoes,
And I'll have all that I need then,
Because I'll have you."

The Goblin King

MAR 10, 2010

I have been alive too long. I've seen too much. I still remember when it was warm, and children laughed and played. I remember when trains ran down these tracks. Now I follow them, one step at a time, hoping that they will lead me back to her. That is my only thought now…just keep following the tracks.

My mother used to tell me stories about the trains. She used to warn me. There were goblins on the trains that would weave their glamour and beguile young girls. The goblin king himself would ride the trains, looking for some young girl to charm, and then he'd tear out her heart and eat it. Fairy tales, I used to think, but now I walk the tracks and I can see the bodies, cold and heartless.

Footstep after painful footstep I follow the tracks, hoping that it's not too late. Hoping that she's still alive. It's been so long, it's taken me years to get here. Gone are the days when one could simply drive to the airport and fly across the sea on a plane. No, I had to walk, the long way round. I have crossed a world to find her, but I made her a promise, and so, finally, I'm almost there.

The cold bites at my bones, my skin is cracked and my joints ache with fatigue and age, but I cannot give in. I keep following the tracks, they led me to her once before, they'll lead me to her again. And then I see him.

Standing in the middle of the tracks up ahead, sword in his hand, and a wicked grin on his scarred face. The goblin king.

Now is not the time to be broken and old, and so all the years melt away from me. My back straightens and I stand tall, as I reach into my coat and find cold, hard steel. I draw my sword and begin to run towards him.

He simply stands there, waiting, that grin fixed on his face, but as our swords meet, I see a flicker of doubt flash in his eyes. Our battle is a dance along the railway tracks, the outcome is never in doubt. As my sword plunges deep within his chest, his life leaves him. He sinks to his knees, black bile spilling from what a man would call his heart, but this creature has no heart.

I leave him there, and set off once again along the tracks. I must find her, I know she's waiting for me.

We still have so much life to live, and there is so much we have yet to see.

The Lizard And The Ketchup

MAR 16, 2010

The lizard and the ketchup,
Met one day,
As the sun shone high in the sky.
They fell in love,
In a haphazard way,
And nobody quite knows why.
"Would you care to dance?"
Asked the lizard of his love,
As the ketchup passed lazily by.
"But of course, my dear,
Let us dance for a year,"
Came the ketchup's laconic reply.
So they danced on a plate,
On their very first date,
'Till the lizard he started to cry,
And the ketchup said, "Love,
Why do you sob?
For your tears quite cause me to die."
"I cry for the left,
And I cry for the right,
For the fear that it's all just a lie.
I cry for the dance,
The magnificent chance,
That our love might just grow wings and fly."
So they danced for a day,

In an elegant way,
'Till the lizard let out a great sigh,
For the chips had appeared.
And he started to fear,
That the time had arrived for goodbye.

Reckless Life

APR 03, 2010

The moon hangs high in the sky and I feel my pulse start to quicken. It's been too long since I last felt this way. In this age of modern marvels, steam trains and horseless carriages, it's too easy to avoid the full moon, and my travels have kept me from its gaze for eight long months now.

"Give in, give in, give in," pounds my heart.

I feel that first, ecstatic rush of adrenaline as the change begins to take hold. Some call it a curse, but they don't understand the sweet embrace of unbridled passion that it brings. My heart is keeping double time now as my blood races through my veins, bringing a sudden rush of oxygen to my brain. This is the only time I feel truly alive, the rest of my life feels like a shadow in comparison, a grey waking dream.

My ears fill with the strange sounds that I'm always surprised to find are coming from my throat. I howl in rapturous pain as my bones crack, lengthen, and reform into new shapes. My muscles and sinews twist, my flesh flows and the hair on my body thickens to fur and as the transformation comes to an end my howls drop to a low growl.

I am ready, alert and I smell blood.

"Freedom, freedom, freedom," my heart cries as I run into the night.

I find her, alone, writing a letter by lamplight. I have longed for this moment for so long. I have dreamt of devouring her these many nights, I have longed for the full moon to set me free, finally I am here, and she is alone…I must not hesitate.

Yet I do…

The beast longs for blood, it longs to feed, to devour, to make her a part of me…but the man holds back. Beast I may be, but I am no animal…

I retreat back into the night to run wild and free through the forests. I wonder, does she hear me? Does she hear me as I cry out her name to my mistress, the moon? Does she pause, pen in hand, and wonder what beast lurks in the darkness? Or does she, perhaps, hear my cry, and secretly return that longing?

I fear that I shall never know.

The Story Machine

APR 09, 2010

"But…what does it do?" He looked at the strange contraption that his friend had just unveiled, a white enamelled metal box, with a prominent coin slot bolted on to the top. It looked old, even though it had only just been built, but it was clear that an old tumble dryer from a launderette had been used as the base for this intriguing machine.

"It's a story machine, of course!" his friend exclaimed. He had that look on his face; you know the one, that look that says "How was that not obvious to you just from looking?" It wasn't obvious, of course, it was absurd.

"A story machine?" he replied.

"Yes, yes, you just put a token in the slot here," his friend produced a shiny metal token from his pocket and inserted it into the coin slot on top of the machine, "and a story comes out, just like magic!" The machine started to whirr and shake.

"But…but…what will the story be about?" he seemed confused.

"About? About?!" his friend cried in exasperation. "My dear friend, I hardly think that matters! It will be a story, a fine tale about this or that or some such, and it will be magnificent!"

"Magnificent? Are you sure?" he wondered. "But…a story requires imagination, invention; it requires that mystical spark of inspiration. You can't just invent a story out of nothing. You can't pull it out of thin air. It's an art form, not a mechanical process that you can automate."

"That is where you are quite, quite wrong," smiled his friend, "for I have done precisely that. No longer will writers have to toil away for hours, crafting their tall tales. No longer will they be forced to live solitary lives, shut away from the world, slaving at their typewriters. No…all they need is this machine, a token, and…job done!"

"But…will the stories be any good?" he asked.

"Good? Good? What does it matter if they're good?! They will be the correct length, double line spaced, formatted perfectly to the publisher's requirements. They will conform to all the rules of writing, perfectly incorporating the three act structure, and so on, and such forth. They will be perfectly written to all objective standards."

"Objective?" he objected. "But literature is an art form, and art is inherently subjective. How can you judge it objectively?"

"Simply, easily, and, besides, you're talking nonsense," his friend stated. "If it was impossible to judge artistic endeavours objectively then every art degree, every creative writing diploma, every qualification in the arts would be completely meaningless, utterly worthless."

"This," he observed, "has ceased to be a story, and now the writer is merely making a point."

"Oh, dear God," his friend threw his arms in the air in exasperation, "you're breaking the fourth wall! You can't do that! That's against the rules!"

"But everyone does it, it's hardly original, or interesting anymore," he shook his head. "This very writer has done it far too many times now; one might suggest he's running out of ideas."

"Oh, please," sighed his friend, "enough with the meta-textual nonsense. See, this is why we need my story machine; it would do away with pretentious nonsense like this. We'd just have good, quality stories."

"No we wouldn't, they'd be just as bad this," he replied.

The machine stopped whirring and a piece of paper was ejected from its base. He picked it up and began to read. "It's called The Story Machine…"

This Moment Keeps Slipping Away

APR 15, 2010

He carefully placed the knives and forks down on the table, adjusting them so that they would be just so. The evening breeze caught his long, dark hair. It was a pleasant, warm, spring night and he thought it would be nice to eat outside for a change. He'd draped fairy lights over the fence and he blinked as their soft, warm light flared on a smudged spot on his glasses. He removed them and rubbed at the smudge with a corner of his shirt.

He looked up at the star filled sky and sighed. It truly was a beautiful, perfect night. He linked his iPod up to a small set of battery powered speakers, and the tinny sound of Peter Gabriel's voice started to waft gently into the air.

He lit the tall, red candle which stood in the centre of the table, so that its soft flame could flicker between them as they gazed into each other's eyes across dinner.

He sat down, everything was perfect. Everything was ready for the most wonderful, romantic evening.

Well, almost everything…

He looked over at the empty chair opposite him and slowly started to cry.

Leaves Of Three

MAY 27, 2010

Leaves of three, let it be.
Hairy vine, no friend of mine.
Raggy rope, don't be a dope!
One, two, three? Don't touch me.
Berries white, run in fright.
Berries white, danger in sight.
Longer middle stem,
Stay away from them.
Red leaflets in the spring,
It's a dangerous thing.
Side leaflets like mittens,
Will itch like the dickens.
If butterflies land there,
Don't put your hand there.

That was a time in the past when things were. Was it? Yes. Perhaps. There was death with a kiss. Forgotten time. Passion. Life. The ever after. Ha! Forgotten truth. Children play, loss of innocence, hatred was there. Quietly lurking in the thicket. Waiting. Watching. Where did they go? Poison souls.

Kiss me with death, with life, with eternity. Smother me in lost spiritual identity with a mask of incredulity. Look for meaning elsewhere, elsewhen. Just words.

Happily she crawls through fields of glass. Flowers crowning her like the death masks of Mycenae. Poison fills her veins like the pain of the rain that fills her eyes. Inspiration drips from her fingers, searing his back with rage.

At last the never is reached. Found. Lost. Regained. Paradise is poison, ever changed, ever lost, ever sought and fought for. But yesterday was here tomorrow and ever shall be. Estranged.

Can you find it? Can you feel it? Did you capture and reveal it? Flows like a river through forever. Their soul is your lie.

If you found it here you did better than me.

Leaves of three, let it be.

What Drives Us

JUL 08, 2010

The wind whipped through his hair, blowing it in his eyes, but he remained unblinking. Fine drops of rain spattered his brow as a grim blanket of thick, grey cloud loomed above him, but he stood his ground. His finger gently caressed the trigger of his standard issue rifle as his gaze remained fixed on the man who stood in front of him.

"Imagine," he said, "a world without war. A world devoid of conflict. Where would we be, the human race? We'd be little more than a band of barely evolved, hairless apes, scrabbling about on the plains of Africa."

"I suppose you're right," the man opposite him nodded slightly.

"Of course I'm right," he continued, "what do you think drove our ancestors out of Africa in the first place? Conflict. It's obvious. Resources ran scarce and rather than share, our forefathers fought over them, and that drove them out of that antediluvian valley. That started our race on a journey of exploration and discovery that's ultimately led us to the moon and beyond."

"So, you're saying that war isn't good for nothing?" the man enquired of him.

"Exactly," he confirmed. "War drives progress, it inspires men to greater things. The rockets of war became the rockets that now drive our exploration of the solar system. War is good, war is great, war is what truly separates us from the beasts of the field."

"But, aren't the beasts happy?" asked the man.

"No, they just are," he replied. "They're neither happy nor sad, they just exist, and that is a state I find anathema to my very being. I cannot countenance mere existence. I want to truly live."

"And killing me will achieve that?" the man asked, although the answer was clear.

"No," he replied.

"No?" The man was surprised.

"I'm killing you because you slept with my wife."

"Oh," the man replied. "Shit."

July

JUL 14, 2010

So, you see, the problem is that it's July.

July? Why is that a problem?

Because things happen in July.

Things? What sort of things?

Oh, everything, really, it's not a good month. It just sits and waits for me with its little surprises. It's fairly evil.

The month of July?

Yes.

The whole month?

Pretty much. So I was thinking about just kinda' going into hiding and putting my feet up for the month, that way it couldn't get me.

And…how's that working out for you?

Not too well, really. Especially as I have that thing this weekend.

Yes, that should be interesting…

That's the problem! July and its…interesting things…

But…sometimes they're good, right?

Well, yes…

So this might be one of those good July things.

I suppose so…

Or at least one of those bad July things that seems really good at the time, but later turns out to have been bad…

Oh, one of those, yeah…

So maybe you should just be excited.

But, July…

Oh, do shut up, stuff happens to you all year…

You have a point.

I always do.

I'll get my coat…

Don't forget the…

I haven't…

Avant Garden

JUL 20, 2010

The soft call and response chirping of a pair of young birds filled the twilight air as he sat on the rough brick steps and looked out across the garden. The light was slowly fading but the warmth of the day still clung to him like the memory of a lost lover. Summer's gentle kiss still stained his lips as he toyed with the half drunk bottle of beer in his hands. He was half drunk himself, but accepted this rare moment of relaxation and let the soothing tide of subtle inebriation wash over him.

Muffled noises came from within the house behind him, but he was only barely aware of them, instead drinking in the peace and solitude of the moment. A gentle breeze blew over him and he closed his eyes, breathed it in deeply and held it. With a long sigh he exhaled, letting the stresses of the last few years pour out of him. Lifting the bottle to his lips he let the beer slip past his lips and down his throat again and for one rare moment he simply existed.

He let go of a past that he'd been carrying around like a dead weight since he was a teenager and gave no thought to tomorrow. For a fleeting instant there was only now.

He almost missed the sound of her footsteps behind him, and if he'd been less relaxed he might have been startled to find her sitting next to him. Her shoulder brushed against his as she leant into him, and the warmth of her body against his made him smile. He felt her hand slip into his and her head rest against his shoulder.

They didn't say a word, they didn't need to. They sat in silence as the sun slowly slipped below the horizon and she held onto him 'till morning.

He placed the bottle down on the step beside him and wondered when the dream would come true.

Fishing With Wotsits

JUL 26, 2010

"I…" he began, with a flourish, as he pranced along the riverside, the vodka having gone to his head a little, "do not understand fishing."

"Really," she laughed, "and why is that?"

He looked her in the eye, trying to seem suave and sophisticated, hoping that the glint in his eye seemed attractive and not cheesy. "Because," he replied, "I can sit at home and not catch fish."

"I think the point is that you actually catch fish," she smiled back at him, the glint in *her* eye was undoubtedly attractive, and he wondered if it had been placed there deliberately or if she just looked at everyone that way.

"No, no, noooo," he continued, acting just a little more drunk than he was in the hopes that it would be endearing, "the point is to sit and get cold. I have been fishing exactly two times in my life, and there was no catching of fish involved on either occasion."

"None at all?" she smiled, and he momentarily lost his train of thought.

"Um…" he stammered for a moment, "no! Admittedly the first time I was using a toy fishing rod and a packet of cheesy wotsits for bait…and there may not have actually been any fish in that stream…but that's besides the point. The second time there was an actual proper fishing pole and actual proper bait, and an actual proper river…"

"An actual proper one?" she laughed.

"Yes!" he exclaimed. "And yet there was still no catching of fish!"

"Actual proper fish?" she asked, giggling lightly.

"Actual…proper…fish…" he nodded in reply.

"So…" she looked thoughtful.

"So," he replied, "that's why I don't like fishing."

"Yes, you do," she said, enigmatically, and skipped slightly ahead of him.

"What?" he asked, a little confused, and quickened his pace slightly to catch up with her.

"You love fishing," she smiled. "You're doing it right now."

He stopped and smiled at her, and simply said, "Oh…"

"And so am I."

Cake Or Death?

AUG 19, 2010

"Hey, cake, I love cake!" he smiled, but who wouldn't? It was, after all, cake, and cake was second only to pie.

"I know you do," she laughed, her eyes sparkling as she enjoyed his giddy, child-like reaction to the treats laid out before him. "Cake or death?"

"Death…no, wait, I meant cake!" They both laughed now, but she could see he was a little distracted by trying to decide exactly which cake to eat.

"So…what are you going to have first?" she asked.

"I fancy a chocolate éclair," he replied, "you know how much I love them… The chocolate, the cream, the pastry, they're just cake perfection. Where's the éclair?"

"There, um, isn't one," she cautiously replied, she'd known this was coming, but, still, he should just be pleased he had cake, right?

"Why is there no éclair? Éclairs are my favourite, why wouldn't you get me an éclair?" he asked, aware that he sounded a little ungrateful, so he tried to say it with a smile and seem endearing.

"Because you can't have an éclair, I know you want one more than anything, I know it's your favourite cake in the whole wide world, but you can't have one," she sighed. "Have another cake, a vanilla slice, a doughnut, a cinnamon roll…"

"But…but…I don't want any of those…"

"They're nice, they're tasty, you'll enjoy them, trust me," she smiled.

"I know, they're great, they're wonderful…especially the cinnamon roll, I can kinda' see myself eating that…but all the time I'd still be wanting the éclair."

"There's a French fancy here, you like those…" she offered him the bright pink cake.

"I just ate one, it left a funny aftertaste…"

"Are we even talking about cake anymore?" she looked puzzled.

"Were we ever?" he replied.

To The Writer Of My Life

AUG 25, 2010

To the writer of my life,

Re: Your recent use of hats.

The fez at the London Film and Comic Con was a nice comedic touch; I think we can all agree on that. Sure, it was a little predictable, but I can't fault your timing. It showed up at exactly the right place and time, and I certainly have no complaints about the price, heh. Not sure that trying to do the fez joke a second time at Auto Assembly really worked, but others were having fun with it…more of a recurring background theme, eh? I think I get what you were going for there.

The red bowler hat today, on the other hand, was a master stroke, seriously. I don't think I'd have thought of that one, and having her be the one to notice it and point it out just made the moment even more heart wrenchingly painful. So thanks for that. The rain, the shared umbrella, all at a moment when not saying those words just wasn't possible anymore probably would have been enough on their own…but adding the hat just before, that was genius.

So, well done, excellent writing…

Now, as a cold, hard rain lashes down against my window through the dark night, I can't help but think…you're veering into cliché now.

I.

I'm Not Drunk

AUG 31, 2010

S'really okay, ah'm fine. Stop lookin' at me like that. You know what I mean, yer always lookin' at me like that, like you know better. Like you know wha's goin' on in my mind. Oooo. I. Am. O. K.

Ah'm jus' a little bit drunk, tha's all. Nothin' to worry about. No, I was'n' cryin', I was just partakin' of the night air. Isa' lovely night, you should go out there. Yes, I know it's rainin', that doesn't mean it can't be a lovely night too, does it?

Why, yes, I will have another vodka, thankyouverymuch. No, I don' think ah've had enough already, I can still feel. Feeling is bad. I don' wanna feel. If I have a few more a' these then mebbe I won' feel nuffink. That'd be nice, eh?

You know, yer really very lovely, I don' know if I've ever tol' you that? Oh, I have? Was ah drunk then too? Yeah, figures. Ah'm crap at bein' honest when I'm sober. Actually, ah'm jus' generally crap. Tha's very kind of you to say, but it's true, I know it is. It has to be true else, you know… Shush. Yer jus' bein' nice, but thank you.

S'okay, tomorrow I'll wake up 'an feel like an idiot, an' prolly text you an apology fer bein' like this. Then

I'll pick meself up, dust meself off an' start all over again…again.

I mean, fuggit, I can't keep rollin' ones, can I? Heh… snake eyes…

Snake Eyes is cool…

The Longest Word

SEP 24, 2010

There are fish here, can you see them? Swimming around in the pond. Look, there's one now. I smile and I run around, jumping over the water at the corners of the pool. It's a grey day, but you get used to that here, and it doesn't really matter. It's time with my mum, just the two of us, and that's all I really care about. I don't even know why we're here or what we're doing, none of that matters.

I barely notice the Swiss cottage, it's not as interesting as the pond. After all it's old, and worn, and I don't care who Charles Dickens is, he sounds boring. Nevertheless, my mother feels the need to tell me about him, that it was his, and the he wrote his last books there, every time. I guess it matters to her. Books are her life after all. Words. She cares about words. She teaches me the longest word there is, and so one day I find myself correcting my English teacher, and telling her that it's floccinaucinihilipilification, and not antidisestablishmentarianism, which is a double negative anyway.

Damn her and her love of words. Now I find myself hunched over a keyboard, trying to form sentences, trying to say something, anything, with meaning. On a Friday night!

I continue this love affair with words, with language, passed on from her. I relish the feel of them in my mouth. I revel in the way they flow from my fingertips. I savour the rhythm of the clicking keyboard.

I lose myself, for a moment, and I'm back there again.

There are fish here, can you see them?

Little Bee

SEP 30, 2010

It was a day, much like any other day, spent talking to friends, as he usually did. Just random communication about nothing of any great importance. He hardly noticed it at first, but nevertheless, there it was, a little bee. It was not any ordinary kind of bee, for a bee would usually make him leap up in fear of being stung. No, this was not a stinging bee (or, at least, he hadn't thought so then, but we may or may not come to that in the telling of this tale). The thing about this bee, that set it apart from the other bees, those stinging, buzzing bees, was its smile. This crazy little bee with its crazy big smile.

A simple request for friendship was made, and accepted, which seemed as nothing at the time, but as the days went on, he began to notice that the bee was always there. No matter where he was, or what he did, everywhere he went, the bee was with him. When he was feeling down, the bee would pick him up, would listen to him ramble on for hours about his woes. The bee would be patient with his delusions, would marvel at his illusions, and almost never say, "I told you so." Mostly, the bee would smile, and make him feel young and wild and free.

The problem was he had started to think of it as his bee. It was silly, he knew, and yet for some reason the words "my bee" floated, unbidden, into his mind and refused to leave. But it was not his bee, it was a wild and untamed thing, and that was, after all, what made it so wonderful.

He was reminded of this, from time to time, as he watched the bee fly away. It would return to him, and not speak of its adventures apart from him, for it could see in his eyes that certain things were best left unsaid. For, after all, every bee has its sting, no matter how reluctant they might be to use it.

So for now he resolved to treasure his time with the little bee, to not complain when it woke him early in the morning with mad tales of bats and canaries. To enjoy the smile, that crazy smile, that always broke like sunshine waves upon his loneliness. For he knew the day would come when his bee would fly away and not return.

No, not his bee.

He kept forgetting that.

The Last Dragon

OCT 12, 2010

I have searched all my life for you,
Scoured the fields,
Ran down the mountainsides,
Still you would not yield,
I have hunted a lifetime,
Travelled this land,
Until the day I held,
The last dragon in my hands.

Scion of the ages,
Son of the wilds,
The wisdom of the universe,
Contained within a child,
Alas we never knew you,
And could not understand,
Until the day we held,
The last dragon in our hands.

Nothing but a dream to us,
Carried on the wind,
A whisper from the darkness,
Of every time we've sinned,
A wicked little melody,
From a half remembered band,
A song I hear now that I hold,
The last dragon in my hands.

Empty Rooms

OCT 18, 2010

"Sit down, Mr Grayson," she said in a firm monotone.

The scrape of the chair leg on the floor echoed as he took a seat in the mostly empty hall. He sat, uncomfortably, not taking off the crumpled, grey trench coat that clearly served him as a second home.

"Um," he began, "what is this?"

She peered at him through thick glasses, taking in the rough stubble on his chin and the shock of short, messy black hair atop his head and frowned. "We just need you to answer a few questions."

"Why?" he asked, scratching his chin, wondering how anyone could be quite so neat and tidy and dull. Her hair was scraped back into the most solid bun he'd ever seen, and her dark grey skirt suit didn't seem to have a single crease in it anywhere.

She smiled thinly and simply said, "This won't take long."

"Okay, fine," he grimaced.

"When did you fall, Mr Grayson?" she asked.

"I...what? I'm sorry, I don't understand the question," he frowned, hard.

"When did you fall, Mr Grayson?" she repeated.

"I don't know what you're talking about," he shook his head.

"When...did...you...fall..."

He sighed, a long, deep sigh.

"When..."

"I didn't so much fall as saunter vaguely downwards," he laughed, quoting one of his favourite books. She was not amused.

"It says here that you were kicked out..." she paused as she flicked through a pile of papers that had been sitting on her lap, "...for falling in love with a mortal."

"Oh, that, yeah..." he shifted uncomfortably in his chair.

"Are you all right, Mr Grayson?" she asked.

"Oh, sure, yeah, it's just hard to get comfortable sometimes, I never did get used to not having the wings," he smiled. She didn't return the smile.

"Did she love you back?" she asked.

"Does it matter?" he looked away, studying the wall to his left intently.

"Did she love you back?" she repeated, coolly, calmly, without a hint of frustration in her voice.

"I…I don't know. She said she did…once…or words to that effect, anyway. I really don't see why it matters now, it was such a long time ago," he sighed.

"Hmm," she said, and wrote something down on her notes. "So how long were the two of you together?"

"Oh, well, it was a long time ago now, I don't remember," he said, failing to keep the hurt off his face.

"A thousand years to the day since you fell, Mr Grayson," she stated plainly.

"Really? That long? I stopped counting after the first two hundred years or so…" he laughed.

"How long were the two of you together, Mr Grayson?" she asked again, just a flicker of her reluctance to make him answer showing on her face.

"You know…you clearly know…" he replied, a mix of hurt and anger filtering into his voice.

"How long…"

"We weren't," he bit his bottom lip and his eyes filled with tears. "Okay? We were never together. Ever. Is that what you wanted to know?"

"I'm sorry…"

"It's okay, it was a long time ago," he shrugged and wiped his eyes. "Look, what's this all about anyway?"

"It's been a thousand years, Mr Grayson, your time is up, you've paid for your crime, you can come back home," she smiled.

"Come back?" he looked confused.

"Yes, we just needed to complete the paperwork, and now you can return."

"But…but…I can't come back," he stammered, "not yet."

"Why not?" she asked.

"Because I still haven't found it. Don't you understand, I may have been thrown out, but I left willingly…"

"Very well, Mr Grayson, you may stay," she replied, "but understand, you won't get another chance to go home."

"That's okay," he smiled. "I know I'll find it, I know it's out there somewhere…"

With that he stood up, the chair legs scraping across the floor again, and walked out of the hall and down the corridor. She watched him go and quietly said to herself, "Then you're a fool, Mr Grayson, but good luck to you."

My Immortal Soul

NOV 11, 2010

It was dark, but the jars glowed with an ethereal purple light which created sinister shadows across the old man's crooked face. He cracked a wicked smile and laughed at Jonathan through the gloom. He tried to focus on the old man's face, rather than the contents of the jars. The things hanging suspended in fluid looked as if they might move and twitch and he felt his skin crawling at the thought of it. The old man smacked his lips together, waiting for Jonathan to say the words.

"So…will it…" he hesitated for just a moment, "…will it work?"

The old man let out a short, sharp laugh before replying.

"Of course it will work," said the old man, "the question is not if it will work or not, it's whether or not you're prepared to pay the price?"

The room fell silent for a moment and Jonathan forced himself to look at the things in the jars, the twisted shapes, like misshapen snakes crossed with the deformed unborn offspring of God only knows what. He felt the bile rise in his throat, but choked it down, swallowed his revulsion and buried it away somewhere deep inside him.

"You can make me immortal?" he asked the old man, wanting to be sure before he took the next step. "I'll live forever?"

"Yes." The old man nodded. "We've been through this many times. The removal of your soul will give you eternal life, but there is a price to pay. That is why you see this wretched form before you, for it is a price I am not willing to pay myself."

"And the price is…" Jonathan began.

"You know the price." The old man cut in.

"That I will never feel again," he finished. "Eternal life without feeling. Numb to everything."

"Yes, yes, that is the price," the old man nodded, sombrely.

"That," Jonathan smiled, "is no price to pay at all. Take my soul, old man."

The Afternoon Before The Morning After The Night Before

DEC 18, 2010

"Well, this is shit," she sighed, slumping down on one of the worn kitchen chairs in the corner of the vineyard, away from where everyone else was having such a lovely time, and kicking over the drink she'd left on the ground by her chair. "Oh, fuck it!"

"Calm yourself," he smiled, "I'll get you another drink."

"Just forget it, it's fine, it's just a drink, I don't care, I want to go home, this is shit," she complained in one breath.

"We can go soon, don't worry," he sighed, "we just need to stay long enough to be polite."

"Guh, I don't know why he even invited me to his stupid wedding," she grumbled. "Did he just want to rub my nose in it?"

"I expect he just thought he was being nice, you are friends, after all," he suggested.

"Friends?! Friends?! Yes…yes, we are, but…you know full well that we're more than that, always have been," she sighed.

"Yes, but you're still friends, and he wanted you here on his happy day, right?" He smiled one of those half smiles you give when you're trying to be reassuring and helpful but know that your words are unlikely to help in any way.

"I…I don't want him to be happy, though, it's not fair," she pouted.

"You don't want him to be happy?" he looked puzzled.

"No, I want him to be fucking miserable until he realises that I'm what's missing from his life!" She smiled as she said this, but it wasn't a very pleasant smile.

"That's…that's not very nice…" he stammered.

"Yeah, well, maybe I'm not very nice," she frowned.

"Don't be silly, you're…" he started.

"Please, let's not go there again, not today," she cut in.

"Yeah, sure, fine," he said as he swallowed his emotions.

"This whole thing is just one big, fucked up mess!" she exclaimed.

"Now, that I will agree with," he smiled. "Look, we're in a vineyard, we're at a party, there is an unlimited amount of free wine…"

"So?" she looked blankly at him.

"So let's get very, very drunk and do things we'll both regret in the morning," he laughed.

"Oh, shush, you," she rolled her eyes at him. "Go get me some more wine!"

"You want a glass of red or white?" he smiled.

"White!" she shouted at him as he walked back towards the party. "And make it a bottle…or three!"

Fly Away From Here

JAN 04, 2011

If we could fly away from here,
Would you take me to the sun?
Would you shine your love upon me,
And make me your only one?
Would everything be forgotten,
If we just ran away,
And hid ourselves away from us,
For forever and a day?
Or would it all catch up on us,
Just like it has before,
Like a wrecked ship of fools,
Washed up upon the shore?
Maybe I'd be better off,
Stranded all alone,
Leaving everything behind,
In my long forgotten home.
But sitting on a foreign shore,
I'm certain I would find,
That everyday I'd hear your voice,
Still whispering in my mind.
I've tried so hard to silence you,
I've travelled far and wide,
But now I know this much is true,
There's nowhere I can hide.

We Have No Fate But What We Make

FEB 15, 2011

"I thought geese were supposed to be white?" queried the young boy of ten, as he tore another piece of bread from the loaf in his bag and threw it out into the water.

"Um, these are Canada geese," said the man sitting next to him on the bench. He was in his mid thirties, although people often thought he was younger. He too, tore a piece of bread from the loaf he'd brought with him and threw it to the geese.

"Canada geese?" the boy asked. "So…do they say 'aboot' rather than honk?"

"You're probably too young and British to be making that joke," the man smiled.

"I can't help it," the boy replied, "I'm just written that way."

"You're definitely too young to be breaking the fourth wall!" the man exclaimed.

"You know, drawing attention to the fact that I'm doing it, and thereby doing it yourself, doesn't make you all clever and post-modern, you know?" the boy replied, sardonically.

"What ten year old use words like 'thereby,' anyway?" the man laughed.

"How do you know I'm ten?" the boy snapped back.

"Because it said so in the narrative," the man replied, smugly.

"Anyway…" the boy sighed, "so these are Canada geese?"

"Yup," the man nodded. "I went to Canada once, you know?"

"And why did you do that?" asked the boy.

"Because I'm an idiot," the man laughed.

"Well, I'm glad we agree on something," the boy smiled, throwing another piece of bread to the geese.

"You know, you're going to make a lot of mistakes in your life…" the man began.

"Oh, here we go!" the boy rolled his eyes.

"What?"

"This is where we get to the poignant message of the piece, isn't it?" the boy frowned. "We've disarmed everyone with some charming and self referential humour, and now we're going to get all deep."

"Well…" the man tried to interrupt.

"No, no," the boy shook his head. "I've had enough of this nonsense. Things just happen. Stop trying to build a narrative out of them. Stop trying to make sense of it all. Just live. There'll be happy times and sad times, but if you try to make sense of it all, you'll go mad."

"That's…" the man paused, "…very wise for a ten year old."

"Well," the boy smiled, "it helps that I'm fictional."

He Smiled

APR 16, 2011

He slumped down in his chair, the weekend had only just begun and already he felt exhausted. Still, the comics were all neatly arranged on the table in a fashion which he hoped would be conducive to sales. He'd done so many of these shows now, but had yet to figure out any kind of pattern or method to selling the damn things. A simple friendly smile could send a potential customer scuttling away one moment, and the next an angrily barked "Buy comics!" would result in a bumper transaction. There was, he had to admit to himself, no rhyme or reason to it.

The hour felt ungodly, although he knew for most people this was a perfectly respectable time to be up and about. His body clock had long since been ruined, leaving him intimately familiar with three in the morning, and a stranger to eight o'clock. Looking about himself he could tell that his fellow stall holders were in much the same plight, and they all appeared to be engaged in various stages of the quest for caffeine.

He wondered what the weekend held, if he'd spend his time feeling lost and slightly out of place in a hall full of people who felt perpetually out of place. He wasn't quite sure where he fitted in here, especially, at an event where the pecking order in his chosen industry was more clearly defined than usual.

BADABEEP BADABEEP

He fished in his pocket for his phone, expecting it to be a twitter alert from his companion for the day, bemoaning the state of London's public transport system, or wondering if eight in the morning was too early to start drinking whisky. Then he saw her name and smiled. He didn't even need to read the message, it didn't matter; just knowing that he'd crossed her mind was enough to make him smile.

BADABEEP BADABEEP

The hall began to fill with people, comics were sold; people came and went in a whirlwind of colour and beards. None of it mattered. He met all of it with a smile.

BADABEEP BADABEEP

He was miles away.

BADABEEP BADABEEP

Just for today.

BADABEEP BADABEEP

He smiled.

The Song Remains The Same

APR 22, 2011

With a loud screech the music came to an abrupt halt.

He dropped the violin to the floor, barely noticing it break in two as it hit the ground.

The song had ended.

He silently left the room, firmly closed the door behind him and began to hum a new tune.

Dinner And A Movie

MAY 04, 2011

"So," he smiled, "where do you want to eat?"

"I really don't mind," she replied, "you choose."

"No, don't make me choose, you know I can never choose." He wore a somewhat pained expression on his face.

"Well, that's true, you do get kind of stuck in a mental loop when faced with any kind of decision," she laughed.

"Oh, shush you," he mockingly scolded her. "Right, seriously now, do you want to eat-eat, or just, you know, grab a coffee and a bite."

"Oh, I could eat," she nodded.

"So, somewhere we can eat-eat," he mused.

"As opposed to just sort of eating?"

"Yes, exactly," he nodded. "So, what do you want? Proper food or something greasy?"

"Something greasy," she laughed, "but we should probably get proper food, I'm getting fat."

He looked at her, a stern, hard look.

"You are not getting fat," he stated. "You are the least fat person I know. I'm fat. You are not."

"No, I've put on weight…" she began.

"Oh, I notice you don't disagree with me being fat…" he huffed.

"Well, you know…" she smiled.

"Fine, fine, fine…" he rolled his eyes. "Let's just keep walking until we find somewhere nice, eh?"

"Oh, you're so decisive," she smiled. "How about pub food?"

"Pub food sounds good to me," he nodded.

"You're paying," she said.

"I like how you never phrase that as a question, you just assume," he smiled, wryly.

"It's because you love me," she smiled, sweetly.

"Yeah, yeah, yeah, just try not to order the exact same thing as me again, people will think we're a couple."

"People already think we're a couple," she shrugged.

"So what do you want to do after dinner?" he asked.

"Oh, you can take me to a movie," she smiled.

Drunken Communications With The Deity

MAY 10, 2011

"Have another glass," she smiled, filling his wine glass once again, "it's not going to drink itself."

"It might, you know," he smiled.

"No, really, I doubt it," she replied, cautiously. "You're a bit drunk, aren't you?"

"Well, you know, maybe, a bit," he laughed. "There were all those other glasses before this one, they've… um…added up…that's it."

"We might as well finish the bottle though."

"But…but…it might drink itself. I mean, quantum mechanics and all that, all possibilities are played out within the quantum multiverse," he nodded, sagely.

"The quantum multiverse?" she asked.

"You…you have very pretty eyes," he smiled at her and blinked.

"Yes, yes…" she said, dismissively. "What about this quantum multiverse."

"Oh, oh that…" he thought for a moment. "You seriously think I can explain it after one…two… some…some bottles of wine?"

"Give it a go."

"Okay, okay," he began, "you know how a photon can, like, be in two places at once, right?"

"No, but I'll take your word for it," she nodded.

"There've been experiments that prove it," he continued, "something to do with a wavy pattern on the wall. Wibbly wobbly patterns of light…"

"But you digress…" she prompted.

"But I digress!" he exclaimed. "So, anyway, yeah, light…photons…can be in two places at once, but the act of viewing the photon determines where it actually is."

"This…this is like that Schrodinger's cat thing, right?"

"Yes! Yes…like the cat. Poor cat. Is it alive or is it dead? Nobody knows… Is it both alive and dead? Maybe…" he pondered.

"And…" she suggested.

"And…and…and…" he stumbled on his words for a moment, gathering his thoughts, "and, yeah, so they reckon now…"

"Who reckon?" she interjected.

"The…er…science people…the quantum mechanics…I don't know…" he frowned. "Anyway, they reckon that the photon is still in both places at once…maybe in many places at once…across the multiverse…and by observing it, rather than forcing it to be in a certain place, you're just determining which universe, across the multiverse, you are in."

"But…that's just photons…" she was struggling to grasp the idea.

"No, no, not just photons, all particles, on a quantum level…I think," he nodded.

"On a quantum level though, we…we're not…like… quantum…though…right?"

"But every atom in our bodies, every atom everywhere, is made up of these quantum level particles…that…that exist in the multiverse… these…these multiversal particles," he hesitated. "Or…er…something like that."

"So…what's true at a quantum level…must also, ultimately, apply to…everything?" she asked.

"Well…yes…" he replied.

"So…every possibility…every variation of existence that could conceivably have ever happened… they…they've all happened…and are happening now?" she mused.

"Pretty much, yes," he agreed.

"So…in one universe…this is all real, and not just in your head?" she asked.

"In one universe…I'm God."

I'm Still Out Here Waiting Watching Reruns Of My Life

MAY 16, 2011

This is the sort of thing I should have done so many times, you know? Really. The twinkling orange lights, the sound of the waves lapping against the pebble beach, the sun slowly creeping below the horizon. That moment when a chill creeps into the air and she curls up into your arms to keep warm. These little fleeting moments, these memories you store, that keep you going.

There's a line in a song I love, about it taking time to heal the broken memories that another man would need just to survive. I have so few of those memories to begin with, and it's hard to enjoy any of them. They always end up tinged with pain and loss, the knowledge of what was to come later. Not that there have been many of them anyway, so few happy days. Sometimes it just seems hopeless, like there'll never be another one, so what's the point, you know? Why keep going?

We should have had these moments, when we were young. She and I. I know…I'm just fooling myself. Pretending like there was some grand destiny. Like it was meant to be but we got it wrong. Foolishly believing that in another world, another time, we got it right. I hate the thought that this is all there is, all there's supposed to be. That I'm meant to be alone.

They all tell me I'm wrong, of course. That there'll be someone. That's what we're told, someday, one day, it will happen. There's always a happy ending. It's not true, of course. Some people die alone. Did they deserve it? Were they bad people? Were they unlovely? Were they impossible to love? No. It just… didn't happen. Then I look at the happy couples, and I wonder…are they really happy or are they just afraid to be alone? How cynical I have become.

There are times when I am happy, and there are times when I am sad, neither last forever, and I know that's how it is for everyone. Happiness is not a place, it's a feeling. I tell myself this over and over again and try to believe it, but my happy place is in your arms, and yet I feel guilty for the stolen moments I spend there.

I am tired, and I feel old, as if the sun is starting to set, and the night is growing cold. My arms are empty and there is nobody here to warm me. All that lies ahead of me is darkness, and I fear that the dawn will never come.

The Dark

MAY 28, 2011

It's very dark down here. I suppose it's supposed to be, it is a cave, after all. Caves are dark, it's in their nature. This is…hmmm…the best way I can describe it is to say that it's stupidly dark, really. I know I shouldn't have wandered off from the tour, but I thought I saw something. It was a flicker of movement, it was…it was definitely something. Someone might have needed help, so I just paused for a moment, really, just to take a look. I thought it would be easy to catch up with everyone else, and I had my paraffin lamp to guide me back to them.

I shouldn't have wandered off, but I saw something, I really did. I shouldn't have gone to look though, that was a really stupid thing to do, but I thought it would be so easy to find my way back. How complicated could it be?

I know I saw something, and…and what was that? I definitely heard something. That was a thing. A definite something. I'm not sure what it was though. It sounded far away. Maybe it was just the tour. Maybe they're looking for me.

It didn't sound like the tour.

The lamp's getting dimmer now, I guess the oil must be running out. There's the sound again. It's getting closer now. It's…it's definitely not the tour.

The lamp's gone out. I'll just wait for my eyes to adjust to the dark, I'll be able to see soon.

There's the sound again. It's here.

I can't see. Why aren't my eyes adjusting?

It's very dark down here.

Despite The War

JUN 03, 2011

So, we'd just spent…you know, I can't even remember how many days it was now…some days…some will have to do. So, we'd just spent some days driving across Europe. We left from Kent in England, hopped a ferry over to France, drove down through France until we got to Italy. Then we drove across the top of Italy and got an over night ferry down to the bottom of Greece. The plan had originally been to get the ferry over to Albania, but we couldn't get permission to do that…there was a war on, after all. So we drove up through Greece. Oh, I remember getting caught up in a military convoy somehow and being shepherded into the port at Thessalonica, where the bus was surrounded by angry looking men with guns. The guy sitting next to me got out his camera and started taking pictures through the window. I think it was at that point that I started seriously thinking we'd at least get arrested, if not shot.

We didn't, of course, we got waved on and continued up through Greece. They have red mountains there. Not some earthy red, not mountains that have a bit of a reddish hue to them. Proper bright red mountains. You know, if you've ever wanted to visit a different world, just travel. There's some amazing stuff to see right here, you know? But I digress…

We travelled up through Greece to the Macedonian border. That's where we were headed, I should have said, Macedonia…or The Former Yugoslav Republic of Macedonia…or FYROM…whichever works for you. The Greeks don't like you calling it Macedonia, because Alexander The Great was from Macedonia, and they like to think of him as one of theirs. The toilets on the border were…interesting… I won't go into too much detail, but I'll just say that I'm not sure how anyone could achieve that effect without standing on their hands and using some kind of sprinkler attachment.

We passed burnt out tanks on the way to Skopje, which was a little unsettling, if I'm honest.

Anyway, yes, we'd just spent some days travelling across Europe, and all any of us really wanted to do was sleep, but the Macedonians are a hospitable people and they insisted on taking us out. You know, even though there was a war on and there were NATO planes flying overhead, popping over the Kosovan border on bombing raids. So, despite the war, and us all being dog tired, we were sitting in a restaurant in Skopje. I forgot to mention that our host had thrown the chef out of the kitchen and insisted on cooking for us himself. So, anyway, yeah, despite the war and being exhausted, we were in this restaurant in Skopje eating the hottest damn chillies you've ever had. We paid for that later that night…boy did we ever pay… But it was amazing, what a night.

They said that the people we took that trip with, those people would always be our friends. That no matter what, the bonds we'd made on that trip would last forever.

The funny thing is, I don't talk to any of them any more…not even the one I married.

Peacock Flavour Crisps

JUN 09, 2011

"I hate meat flavoured crisps!" he complained. "What flavour are these anyway?"

"Peacock."

"Peacock? Peacock flavour?" he spluttered. "What... what kind of flavour is peacock?"

"It's peacock flavour," she replied, "that's what kind of flavour it is."

"But...but who knows what a peacock tastes like?" he asked.

"Someone who's eaten peacock," she replied, matter of factly, adding a quick, "Duh."

"Do people eat peacocks?" he wondered.

"Well, they must do, mustn't they," she said, "else there wouldn't be peacock flavour crisps."

"I've never eaten peacock," he stated.

"Well, you wouldn't have, would you," she explained, "peacocks fancy food like what rich folk eat."

"Peacock's fancy food!" he exclaimed. "That's just silly."

"Eat your crisps."

"I don't want to," he sulked. "Stupid peacock flavour crisps…"

"Fine, I'll have them," she said, exasperated, "you have the velociraptor."

The Threads Of Destiny

JUN 15, 2011

The distant rumble of the ship's engines were all that filled his ears as he slowly worked his way to the control room. This was it; this was the moment they'd all waited for, the moment that a life time had been building towards. They'd finally left the Sun's gravity well and could fire up the inter-stellar engines. They would be the first people to venture out of our solar system, cross the vast, empty blackness of space, and visit another star system.

The door to the control room opened with a loud thunk, and he simply acknowledged his crew mates with a nod as he took his place in the forward control chair.

"This is an auspicious day," he said quietly and calmy. "This project united the people of Earth in our darkest hour. The human race finally set aside their differences and came together to make this happen, to achieve this dream. It was for this very moment that world peace was created."

He powered down the in-system engines and a deathly silence fell within the control room. The only sound was the collective steady breathing of the six members of the crew.

"Ramirez, fire up the inter-stellar drive and take us to the stars," he said.

The man known as Ramirez flicked several switches in a sequence he'd rehearsed many times over the last decade. Then, pausing only to draw a deep breath, he pulled a large and solid looking lever.

Nothing happened.

Not a thing.

They exchanged worried glances, each hoping that the other would think of some obvious reason why nothing had happened yet. Each hoping that someone else would reassure them that this was quite normal, that this was what was supposed to happen.

Finally, he spoke, "Well…something's wrong…"

"We should send a message back to Earth, ask for help…guidance…" suggested Ramirez.

"It would take six months for the message to get there, and another six months for the reply to get back, if we're going to fix this, we'll have to do it now, by ourselves. I'll go and take a look at the drive…"

"But…but that is forbidden…" stammered O'Reilly.

"Yes, I understand that, but what choice do we really have?" he replied. "We either try to fix this ourselves, or we die, here, floating at the edge of the solar system. The in-system drives have been shut down, they can't be restarted and if we can't get the inter-stellar drive working then we'll just stay here forever."

With that he stormed out of the control room, through the labyrinthine corridors of the star ship. Through doors he'd never been through before, with increasingly ominous warnings about what would happen to the crew if they ever passed through them.

Eventually he reached the access hatch for the inter-stellar drive. A small door that housed the control panel that would tell him what had gone wrong. He only hoped that he'd be able to fix it. He prayed it was something simple. A loose connection. A switch that needed flipping. A fuse that needed replacing.

He opened the hatch and in front of him saw a small piece of twine hanging from a hook, and below it a small note which read:

"We're so sorry, we sincerely thought that we could build an inter-stellar drive, but in the end it simply proved to be beyond science. No engine could take you to the nearest star before you were long dead. Building what

we had designed would have bankrupted the newly formed world government, and the resulting economic turmoil would have fractured the fragile peace amongst all humankind that had been achieved while working on this project. The people needed hope, and cancelling the launch would have robbed them of it. Thank you so much, on behalf of the entire human race, for what you have done for us. We are not heartless, however, you have a choice to make. On the wall behind you is a hidden panel, open it and you will find a switch that will restart the in-system drives, and you can return home, if you wish. Again, thank you so much."

He quietly closed the hatch and turned around. He found the hidden panel, opened it, restarted the in-system drives and began the long walk back to the control room.

He smiled as he walked through the door, and nodded to his fellow travellers.

"Point the ship to the stars," he said. "We have a long journey ahead of us."

The Loss Of The Ether Sprite

JUL 15, 2011

Rain lashed down through the planet's turbulent atmosphere, and despite being sealed within a temperature controlled enviro-suit, Harry Swanson couldn't help but feel a shiver run down his spine. He watched his partner, Jenkins, struggle to find his footing on the narrow ledge they were traversing. The enviro-suits protected them from the weather but limited their visibility. It was a trade-off that was usually worth it, but here and now he sorely wished that removing the helmet was an option. Even with the helmet on, though, he could clearly see that the terrain disappeared sharply into what looked like oblivion, just scant inches from where he was stood. "Watch it, Jenkins, you're…" he began, but it was too late. Time seemed to stop for an instant as his partner lost his footing, then everything sped up beyond normal time and he was gone, a faint scream echoing over Harry's com unit as he disappeared into the mist below. Harry stuck out his chin to switch channels on his com. "Ether Sprite this is Swanson, I've lost Jenkins, ma'am."

"Swanson this is Ether Sprite," came a female voice over the speakers in his helmet, "what do you mean you've lost Jenkins?"

"He, ah, lost his footing," Harry explained, "appears to have plummeted to his death. Nasty business."

"Yeah, well, you need to find him and bring back his identi-chip," sighed the female voice over the comm. "Without that I'm going to have a ton of paperwork to fill in when we get back to Earth, and I'll be holding you personally responsible for that."

"What?" Harry complained.

"Swanson…I will find some way to deny you your bonus if you don't get me that identi-chip, you hear me?"

"Yes, ma'am," he sighed.

He clumsily fished out the light weight rope from his back pack. It was made of millions of nano-filament cords wound together into an exceptionally light but incredibly strong rope. Fixing it securely, he hoped, to a rocky outcrop, he began to carefully rappel down the cliff face after Jenkins. It was an exceptionally long drop, and the ledge he'd begun his descent from soon disappeared into the mist above him. Eventually his feet found solid ground; he pulled out his torch and began to search for Jenkins' body in the gloom.

Thankfully it wasn't long before he found it. The faceplate on Jenkins' helmet had a rather large crack running down the middle of it, so if the fall hadn't killed him (and judging by the nasty angles in his spine and neck it almost certainly had) the noxious nature of the planet's atmosphere would have done for him fairly quickly anyway.

With a sigh he retrieved the identi-chip from Jenkins' helmet, reflecting for the briefest moments on the fact that the people he worked for didn't care about recovering the body, but only minimizing the amount of paperwork involved in someone dying on the job. It was not comforting to know that his death was, one day, likely to be no more than an annoying inconvenience to someone in middle management.

It was as he was tucking the identi-chip into a pouch on his leg that he noticed them.

"Ether Sprite, this is Swanson, I've got something here…" he began.

"It had better be that damn identi-chip, Swanson," the female voice replied.

"Yeah, sure, I've got that, but forget about Jenkins for a minute, I've found something…" he continued.

"What have you found now, Swanson," the voice sighed.

"Well…it looks like some eggs…maybe half a dozen…" he replied.

"You planning on making an omelette, Swanson?" the voice snapped back, sarcastically.

"Will you just shut up for a minute, Christy, I'm serious here…I have eggs…*alien* eggs…as in life, Jim, but not as we know it…" his voice gained a slightly forceful edge to it.

"Harry, are you serious?" Christy replied.

"I'm damn serious," he shot back at her. "You want me to bring them in?"

"Of course I want you to bring them in," she replied. "But I'm getting fifty percent."

"Thirty."

"Forty percent and you get to take me to dinner."

"You're on."

* * * *

"So, what do we do with them?" Christy mused.

"Well, we can't risk them hatching or something on the trip home…" Harry began.

"No way," Christy cut in, "I think we've all seen *those* movies."

"Jenkins' stasis pod is empty," said Harry, deep in thought. "I say we stash them in there for the ride home, then hand them over when we get back to Earth and split the reward that our generous corporate benefactors are bound to shower upon us."

"Sounds like a plan to me," Christy smiled. "What could possibly go wrong?"

* * * *

The Ether Sprite slid silently through the endless void of deep space, inter-stellar engines burning brightly as they warped space around the ship, enabling them to cruise at speeds greater than light speed. Deep inside the ship its crew slept, their metabolisms slowed to a point just next to death by the stasis pods they slumbered within, practically halting the aging process during the months or years spent on inter-stellar voyages.

In one such stasis pod, bearing the identifier "Jenkins – M," a half dozen strangely patterned eggs gently trembled from the vibrations caused by the ship's giant engines.

One of the eggs began to crack…

No girl. Go.

AUG 26, 2011

Moneymoneymoneymoneymoney.
Need money. Gotta get out. Gotta get out of here.
Get away. Too much thinking, too many thoughts,
get somewhere quiet, somewhere away.
Grab the keys, grab the cash, grab the girl. No girl.
Okay, just gogogo.
Keys in the car, pedal to the floor, music on LOUD.
Go.
Gogogo.
Night lights, street lights, fly by, fly away. Gotta
get gone.
Get away.
White lines flying under the car. Eating miles.
Eating thoughts.
Awayawayaway.
Never.
Look.
Back.
Leaveitallbehind.
Flee!
Grab the keys, grab the cash.
Grab the girl.
No girl.
Go.

Tangled

SEP 01, 2011

It's strange how it happens, really. Just out of the blue, you'll see a picture of someone on a website; or you'll just randomly start talking to a friend of a friend on some social network somewhere; or you'll just talk to someone in passing at some event somewhere, just like you talk to a thousand other people like that and never, usually, speak to them again.

Before you know it they're a part of your life, they're on your mind every day. You see them, you hang out, and they're no longer some random person, they're no longer just some person you met once, they're *important* to you. They matter.

I mean, sure, we lie and say that everyone matters, that everyone is important, and to a certain extent that's true…but that guy you just cut up on your way home from work isn't important to you, or that girl you were rude to on the bus. Only a few people really matter to us, to us as individuals.

We like to think it's a conscious choice we make, but it's not. It creeps up on us. After all, they were just someone we shared a smile with once, or we thought had nice eyes. Now, however, we have that gnawing ache inside us because they're not there, and we find ourselves saying things like, "Somehow it feels like I've known you forever."

We don't choose this. None of us would ever choose this. We want to make our own way through life, to follow our own distinctive path. Yet one day it happens, and we look back, and the path is all tangled up with all these other people's.

It's all a horrible, complicated mess, but that's life. That's the point of it all, really.

To get tangled up.

Degeneration

SEP 19, 2011

It took a while to build the shelter, but we knew we didn't have much time, so it's nothing fancy. Not much more than a big brick box, really. Those were scary days, we'd seen the first reports on the news after it happened, but after a couple of days the airwaves went dead, so we had no idea when it would reach us. We just knew it would.

Dad used to drive up out of the valley to look and see if he could see any sign. One day he didn't come back, and we knew then that it was time. We sealed ourselves in. We had as much tinned food as we could store, all looted from the local supermarket. Everyone else in the town had fled during those first few days, before the TV went off air, while we were still building the shelter. Mum raided the local gun shop. So we could keep a few shot guns handy, and she even grabbed a cross bow. I'm not sure why. She just said it was cool and she had a strange look in her eye. Of course, we knew that if they got in it would be over, the guns…the crossbow…they were just there so we could go down fighting. Or end it quickly if one of us…you know…

The first night after we locked the door wasn't too bad. There were a few bumps in the night, a few strange noises. Nothing too out of the ordinary when you've grown up on a council estate. I hadn't expected the collapse of civilisation to sound like an ordinary Friday night.

It got worse after that. We could hear the moaning all night, hear them scratching at the walls. You could feel it...taste it...in the air. The need. The hunger. The longing.

By the third week we were just desperate to leave. Desperate to see the sky again. Desperate for a functioning toilet. None of us had slept properly in days, the noises at night were becoming unbearable. We even heard them moving on the top of the shelter; God only knows how they climbed up there.

It was towards the end of the fourth week that mum turned one of the shot guns on herself. She'd just stuck the barrel in her mouth, somehow pulled the trigger, and blown her brains up the wall. I ran through to her the minute I heard the shot, but it was too late. I just stood there numbly, watching her body twitch and wondering what the hell I was supposed to do with the body. Of course, after a month of nothing but tinned food there really was only one thing we could do.

I think it was maybe week six...or early in week seven...that the noises stopped. It wasn't until week eleven that we finally went outside though.

It was hard, it was horrible, it was the worst time of my life. But at least I survived. At least I didn't become one of *them*. An animal.

A Message From Yesterday

OCT 07, 2011

Hello? Hello? Is this thing on? Can you hear me? I'm afraid something terrible has happened. I've…I've gone and got myself a little lost, you see? I should have been here yesterday and, well, I am, it is yesterday, for me. Unfortunately for you, it's today. I think I've hooked the vocal modulator up to the quantum flux decoupler correctly, and routed everything through the tachyon emitter…oh, and then reversed the polarity of the neutron flow…of course… But there's no way to know if it's worked. I could be talking to myself here!

Anyway, if by some miracle of fate you can actually hear me, please go into my study. There you'll find a big box with lots of flashing lights on it. It should be making a whirring sound. If it's not making a whirring sound then we're in trouble. Anyway, assuming it's working, press the big red button. The big red one. Not the green one. Definitely not the…

…no, wait. Silly me. Press the the big green button. Ignore the red button entirely.

Do that and everything should sort of just pop back. Ping! Well, ping back… Ping? Pop? Spring? Yes, spring back, that's more like it. Everything should spring back, and I'll be there and not here.

Hello?

Hello?

The green button…

Or was it the red one?

Technical Support

OCT 13, 2011

Hello? Hello, yes, I've been trying to reach technical support. What do you mean they've blocked my number? I wasn't rude and abrasive, I… Yes, okay, I do apologise for saying *that*, but could I talk to a manager, please? Oh, I *am* talking to a manager? Splendid. The trouble? It's my phone, you see it was eaten by a killer whale and I want to know what you intend to do about it. No, I don't see how it was my fault. No… No… You're misunderstanding me completely. No. Listen. Listen. To. Me. I was *not* at an aquarium. Or by the sea. Or near any large body of water. I was at home. In my living room. A message came up, asking if I wanted to update the software on my phone. I tapped "Yes." The next thing I know…eaten by a killer whale. Yes. Yes, I know how it sounds. Yes, I can assure you that my household is usually killer whale free. No, I'm not going to ask my neighbours, I'm fairly confident that their households are generally killer whale free too. No, I'm not going to ask them. No. So what are you going to do about it? Hello? Okay, I'll hold. Sigh. Ah, there you are! A known issue with that model? A *known issue?* Really? This has happened before? Right, so you'll replace my phone. No, that wasn't a question. Excuse me? Yes,

WORDS ON A WALL

of course I accepted the terms and conditions. No, I didn't *read* them. Nobody reads them! There were sixty seven pages on a tiny phone screen, of course I didn't read them! Oh, you do, do you? Really? So, you're telling me that if there was a clause in there allowing you to sacrifice my first born to the chaos god Nurgle then there'd be nothing I could do about it? *Really?* Clause eighty seven, sub-section twenty eight, paragraph fourteen C? Yes, I can see that it *would* be hard to find willing sacrifices for the great horned one otherwise. Anyway, my phone? You can offer me a replacement for a small handling fee? Well, I suppose that'll have to do then. And can you guarantee me that this one won't be eaten by a killer whale? Right, I didn't think so. But you *can* offer me a plan that includes unlimited texts. Oh, why not then. By next Tuesday. Fine. And my first born? Yes, I'll be sure to anoint him with oil first. Thanks. You too. Goodbye.

Ode To A Tiny Box

DEC 12, 2011

Bored
Bored bored bored bored bored
What to do? Anything, everything and nothing all at
once
Is this a dagger which I see before me?
No, it's a pencil
Take stupid pictures and post them to the internet
I have a Coke bottle on my head
Amuse me, be amused by me, just be
No, don't just be, there's more
Wait, I was wrong, there's…

Not.

For Once

JAN 17, 2012

Come on, the sun is shining,
Come sit by the pool with me,
The sky is blue,
I know you're stressed,
But just relax,
Be a fool, just for once.

Come on, just for a day,
Or two, or maybe three,
I'm so blue,
I know you're happy,
It's not fair,
Be with me for once.

Come on, remember me,
I'll hold my breath,
'Till I turn blue,
Just to make you talk,
To me,
And not her for once.

Come on, the sun is shining,
Come sit by the pool with me,
The sky is blue,
And all that's left,
Is I'm sorry,
And I'm the fool for once.

The Case

JAN 23, 2012

Steve stepped out of the taxi, relieved that he'd made it to his destination in one piece as the vehicle's body work seemed to be at least fifty per cent rust. As he slipped out of the car door he handed the driver a wad of notes, the local currency, he hadn't got the hang of it yet but the driver seemed more than happy and drove off without proffering any change. He breathed in, deeply, immediately wishing that he hadn't as his mouth filled with the flavour of unregulated industrial growth. The tang of sulphur in the air was unmistakeable and he was already looking forward to returning to his air conditioned hotel and steam cleaning himself in the shower.

He looked up at the building in front of him, covered with indecipherable pictograms. He might as well be in ancient Egypt looking at hieroglyphs for all the sense any of it made to him. He allowed himself a brief moment to ponder the fact that you didn't actually have to leave the planet to gain the sense that you were in an utterly alien place. Indeed, he felt more at home in some of the Martian cities than he did here, in the smog filled streets of the Chinese Empire's second city.

Still, he had a job to do, he'd hardly come here for his own amusement, and so he might as well get on with it. The sooner he started, the sooner he'd be done, and yet he still hesitated. The sun's hazy disk was barely visible through the smog, but he could tell it was getting low in the sky, and the last thing he wanted to do was end up stuck in this part of town after dark. Yet still, he paused, and the knot in his stomach that had been ever present since he'd set food in the country tightened just a little bit more. Time was getting on though, and it was too late to turn back, so he reluctantly willed one foot in front of the other and moved towards the door.

The lobby of the building provided respite from the foul tasting atmosphere, but the heavily filtered and stale air inside was only slightly more pleasant to breath. The desk clerk flicked his eyes up to greet him as he stepped in, he was expected, he knew. The clerk simply nodded towards some basic chairs by the lobby's back wall and returned to blankly staring at a small bank of monitors which displayed the feeds from various security cams located in and around the building.

He took his seat; the knot tightening further, this was it.

A middle aged businessman in a tired looking suit emerged into the lobby from a door that led deeper into the building. The businessman nodded at him, and told him, in heavily accented English, to come with him. Steve followed him through a maze of corridors, notice boards filled the walls, all filled with memos and notes he couldn't read. He wondered what lurked behind each of the closed doors they passed, never once did they encounter another person on their way to the businessman's office.

Eventually they reached their destination and the businessman ushered Steve into a cramped and cluttered office. Shelving groaning with files, folders and boxes lined the walls, and the desk was covered in paperwork, empty drinks cans and the occasional item that Steve could only assume held some kind of personal significance to the businessman. Atop a flat screen computer monitor sat a small holoprojector displaying an image of two young children, presumably the businessman's. Steve mentally noted that the office was devoid of any evidence of the existence of their mother.

The businessman sat and motioned for Steve to do likewise. Pleasantries were exchanged, Steve was asked how his flight had been and if he'd had trouble finding the offices. Both men, however, were clearly eager to get down to business, and Steve soon brought the pleasantries to an end by simply asking, "The device, you have it?"

"You have the money?" the businessman asked in return. With that Steve fished a small touchscreen, hand held communication device from his jacket pocket. He noticed a flicker of nervous emotion cross the businessman's face as he reached into his pocket, and realised that he was not alone in being uncomfortable with skirting this close to the edges of the law. He thumbed through the menus, clicked a few onscreen buttons and smiled.

"On the contrary, now you have the money, I think you'll find." Steve tried to seem confident, and found himself relieved that his voice hadn't cracked during that exchange, as his throat had become impossibly dry. He eyed the drinks cans jealously and, remembering a vending machine he'd noticed outside the building on his way in, knew what the first order of business would be as soon as he left.

The businessman turned his attention to the flat screen monitor in front of him, it too had a touchscreen, and after a few swift gestures he smiled broadly, pleased with the new balance of his bank account. "Indeed I do, and so you'll be wanting this…"

The businessman reached under his desk and produced a hefty metallic case with thick rubber corners. He handed it across the desk to Steve.

"You don't mind if I…" Steve began.

"By all means," the businessman replied. "You'll find that everything is in order."

Steve flicked open the latches on the metallic case, and slowly lifted the lid. The room was bathed in a cold blue light, and he smiled softly to himself.

"Oh yes," he said, "this will do, this will do nicely."

Distant Dreaming

FEB 04, 2012

It was simple, really, just find your flight on the board and go to the gate, but there were so many destinations and so many numbers. Even when she found the right number, the right destination and the right departure time she still felt unsure of herself. As she walked through the spaceport, regularly checking her jacket pocket for her passport and tickets, which on the umpteenth inspection were indeed still there, she kept giving the people around her sideways glances, hoping for some confirmation that they were headed in the same direction as her.

She was booked on a relatively short flight, in system, to a colony on one of Saturn's moons. Dione to be precise. However the spaceport was a main travel hub, connecting people to destinations across that quadrant of the galaxy. To the gas mines of Betelgeuse, to the ruins of the first colonies of Epsilon Eridani, to the pleasure parks of Alpha Centauri, as well as multiple in system destinations from Mercury to Eris. As such it was a bustling hive of activity, the air filled with innumerable strange accents, and every one of them carrying the worried tones of the slightly confused.

She'd done this trip before, of course, several times, but it didn't stop her worrying. What if they changed something? What if she'd made a mistake with the booking? What if they didn't let her on the ship? How would she let the people who would be waiting for her at the spaceport on Dione know that she wouldn't be there? It was all irrational, of course, and part of her knew that. With every step her anxiety subsided, with each part of the process, checking in, getting through security, finding the correct boarding gate, her confidence grew. As she finally took her seat on the relatively small and cramped short range ship she allowed herself to relax, pulled out a battered e-reader, and tried to lose herself in an old novel.

As the crew went through the usual pre-flight checks, she found herself lazily gazing out of the window at the big, interstellar ships as they slowly maneuverered in the cramped confines of the busy spaceport on their way to and from the terminal buildings. Every few minutes one of them would thunder in and out of the arrival and departure lanes bringing people from all corners of the galaxy to the birth place of mankind. She knew there were many amazing sights to be seen out there in the star studded blackness of space, but for now she was content to spend a few days in the shadows of Dione's ice cliffs, snuggled up inside a warm apartment with someone she missed dearly, and keeping the cold at bay as they generated their own heat. She realised she was blushing at the thought and turned away from her idle window gazing and back to the book she'd been trying to finish for weeks. At least now she'd have time to just sit and read. Guilt free reading time, shut on a space ship with nothing else she could possibly do.

She felt the ship decouple from the terminal building and the scenery outside the window began to slowly move. She felt the gentle hum of the engines through her seat, and could feel the vibrations start to build as the pilot began to cycle the power up for inter planetary flight. She gripped the arms of her chair nervously, knowing that this was one of the most dangerous parts of the flight, take-off and landing were when the very few accidents that happened tended to occur. At the same time she softly smiled, knowing that she was finally on her way, there was no turning back now, and the next time her feet would touch solid ground she'd be on that distant moon with the woman she loved.

Texting & Scones

FEB 16, 2012

It's never easy, you know, trying to capture a moment. Or, rather, capturing a moment and then fictionalising it, so it's not really about you, and yet still is. Turning a fragment of your life into a universal moment that everyone can identify with, hitting that precise balance between what is specific and personal and what can apply to everyone, it's a tricky business. Then you have the worry of being too specific, especially when people who know you are going to read the words you write and lend them an extra level of significance because why else would you have written them?

This brings us to the pier, and the times I've spent on there. Or, rather, one particular time. Not that it actually holds any great significance, I suppose. It was a windy day, and she'd foolishly worn a hat, which made her seem the spitting image of Romana from Doctor Who. In retrospect, therefore, a walk along the pier might not have seemed like a good idea, and it was far from a "lovely day" but, it was there, and we were there, and so we did. We talked about things, but that's what we do, really. We go to interesting places and talk. I find it strange that people don't talk, but then looking back on my past, there were times when I didn't. Well, there were words, but I rarely actually said what was on my mind. I blame myself for that, really, as much as I was just trying to keep the peace, and keep someone else happy, in the end it just made everyone miserable. There was guilt involved, of course, and religion, but I should have known better.

This is, I think, what my life should always have been – visiting interesting places with wonderful people and talking a lot about things. It took me until my thirties to realise that, and getting on to my mid-thirties too. You have all these drives and urges telling you what you should really be doing when, ultimately, the best things in life are good company, good conversation and interesting places. So I've been doing more of that, not just piers, but libraries and cemeteries, and a lot of central London. You really can never tire of central London; it is a genuinely magical place.

But I digress, of course, frequently and with wild abandon. To return to the pier, it's not likely to slip from my mind, because we had texting and scones, which might not mean much to some, but means a lot to me. It's an odd little thing we have, I expect the Greeks had a word for it, but texting and scones sums it up perfectly for me.

Gedaway

FEB 22, 2012

Fnarg! Gowan, geddout! Geddouttaheyah! S'my place, s'not yours. Goway! I will gnaw on my own entrails if I so please, madam! You look at me with all your judgety eyes, well, tha's why I cameded here, innit? To gedaway! No, no, I will not eyeballs my legs. I think it's highly rude of you. No, in fact, not rude, pineapples, that's what it is. Udderly. You and all of your ears and your fingers, think you can tells it what to do. But it's not so simples, is it? Yuffly.

I would hope that you would consider my feelings in the matter, my fine and most crumbled sir, but I doubt highly that your sofa would allow it, no? Don't shake your head. Or nod it. Or dance a jig. Wait, no, do dance a jig. Dance the finest jig of your life. With a hand bag woven of the finest duck hair.

And they said I couldn't write. Ha! All I needed was the special alonely time. No…don't look in the cupboard, you won't like what you see there. It's my head you see, full of weevils. My eyes were itchy so I scratched them, now my hands are bleedy and it's hard to see. Nails as hard as thighs, you understand? No, you hear, you listen with your ears again, but you don't listen with your thoughts, and so you don't understand. Knowledge without understanding, worthless, you see. Just empty headed know-it-alls. Tha's all you ever were.

Cleanliness Is Next To Godliness

FEB 28, 2012

"Cleanliness is next to godliness, or so they say. I've been next to godliness though and there's nothing clean about it. It's filthy, dirty, stained," he would have laughed, but instead he frowned. It should have been a joke, but it didn't come out like that.

"Stained?" she looked a little shocked. "That's a bit harsh, isn't it?"

"Stained is an appropriate word, I think, because it sticks with you." He frowned a little, gathering his thoughts. "If working behind the scenes at a theatre destroys the magic of show business for you, then just imagine what a peek behind the curtain at a church does for your soul. Deception, that's another good word for it. The deception of others isn't the worst of it though; it's the deception of self that stains your soul."

"In what way, though?" she replied. "Can't someone just have genuine faith?"

"No, not within organised religion," he shook his head, "not if they're truly intelligent. It's necessary for any intelligent, free thinking person to enter into a Faustian bargain based on self-delusion when seeking to make a living while working at a religious institution. I know, I know, that's a deeply offensive statement to most people, but look at it this way…how many of the core beliefs of any given religion can you, as an intelligent human being, honestly accept as literal truth?"

"Literal truth?" she laughed and shook her head. "Why literal truth? Why does that matter? Why not allegory or metaphor?"

He sighed, a long, deep, world weary sigh, "because to work within organised religion you will be dealing with people, on a daily basis, who accept the most ridiculous things as literal truth. Not only that, but it will be your job to accept that. No, not just accept that, but to actively sell these notions to them as literal truth."

"But why?" she was still confused. "Why not teach them that religion interprets the world through allegory and metaphor? Why not explain that it's attempting to enlighten its followers, to give them a deeper understanding of the human condition, to explain something to ourselves about our basic nature; rather than presenting a scientific, literal version of actual factual events?"

"Because most people can't and won't understand that," he explained. "It's easier and more comforting to believe that it's literal truth."

"So why does that make it dirty?" she asked, craftily steering him back to his original point. "What's so unclean about it?"

"It's a lie," he replied, simply. "It's a lie told for personal gain. It starts out innocently enough, you start out believing that you're called of God and doing the right thing, but ultimately you end up lying to people."

"Why?" she seemed sad. "Why not just tell them the truth?"

"People don't want the truth," he told her. "People want a nice, comforting lie. So you tell it to them, and they give you money. And then you realise that you can specifically tailor the lie so that they will give you more money. Before you know it you're in this unspoken conspiracy to part vulnerable people from their cash. You never say it, you never so much as articulate the thought, but deep down you know it's true. And it sticks with you, that lie. It sticks with you knowing that people struggled to get by each month because they were giving money to a lie you sold them. That people left friends and family behind because you promised them that things would get better if they clung to an untruth."

"So why not just tell them the truth?" she asked.

"Oh, I did," he smiled, although his eyes were filled with sadness. "In the end."

"And what happened?"

"They hated me for it."

Ten Green Bottles

MAR 05, 2012

Ten green bottles,
And the little one said,
One man went to mow,
And they all rolled over,
And his dog, Spot,
Sitting on the wall.

It all merges together. After a while, it just becomes this amorphous glob of things in your head. Memory, that is. We were on a bus, a coach, rather, although try explaining the distinction between a bus and coach to a foreigner, that's fun! Anyway, we were on a coach, a school trip to somewhere, and we were singing one of those songs, or all of them, or some of them, and maybe more. The point being, it was a happy memory. I can't really remember where I was, or who I was with, or where we were going, or what we were singing, but we were having a great time. Me and…and…well, the people I was with. I mean, sure, I could infer who must have been there, I could recall certain names of class mates who, really, when I consider it, must have been there. But that's not remembering, that's assumption. It's guess work, really. Educated guess work, but guess work nonetheless.

They say that truth is stranger than fiction, but there's a point at which they blur. They become intermingled, indistinguishable from each other. I'm not talking about some kind of Orwellian double speak here, the political bending of the truth so that the lie, if repeated enough, seeps into the collective consciousness of a nation and simply becomes the truth. "The country is broke," when repeated enough, despite its utter absurdity, becomes truth, accepted unquestioningly by the Luddite masses. Wait…I said I wasn't talking about that, didn't I? I'm talking about those anecdotes that we repeat over and over again, that change and evolve over the years with each retelling. Then, one day, we meet up with someone else who was actually there, and they remember everything in a completely different way, and you're no longer sure what the truth is any more.

That's what I'm talking about, the way your memories swirl together over the years, they mix and ultimately coalesce into a version of the truth that suits us. A version of reality that forms a convenient narrative that provides entertainment at dinner parties or, more importantly, that simply helps us sleep at night. Because it makes sense.

What scares us the most, perhaps, is the truth. The real truth. Not the half-truths and the outright blatant lies we tell ourselves to help make sense of the random and often cruel string of events that make up our lives. We need to believe in stories, not works of fiction, but true stories about ourselves. We need to believe that there's a beginning, a middle and an end. A happy ending.

But if one green bottle should accidentally fall…

In The Black Room With White Curtains

MAR 17, 2012

If you want to hide something then the very best place to put it is in plain sight. Do you have a vast store of ancient wisdom that you want to keep safe for several millennia? Then put it under a giant carving of a man lion, and set that in front of three enormous pyramids that are aligned so precisely that modern construction techniques would have trouble replicating that degree of accuracy. Likewise, if you want to protect the guardians of that ancient knowledge from scrutiny by the public then you do not locate their headquarters behind a hidden door at the end of a secluded alleyway. No, you place it within a plain black building with no discernible markings outside. The sort of place that screams out that it is the forbidden repository of esoteric knowledge and regular venue for clandestine goings on. Why? Simply because the human mind is a wonderful thing which has the astounding propensity to reject the most obvious explanation for anything. We crave complexity, we hunger after mystery, so when presented with a simple and obvious explanation we denounce it as too easy, and keep looking for the answer.

Hiding in plain sight is what we do best, and we've been doing it for thousands of years. You know where we are, if you think about it right now, you'll know where to find us. We're in that building that you've always wondered about but have consistently dismissed your wonderings as silly. They're not silly, the only reason that nobody has investigated those very same thoughts which you suppress every time you walk past us is simply that they think exactly the same thing as you – it's too obvious, someone would have investigated by now, somebody would know. The children know, they whisper it in the playground, they hold their breath as they walk past us, and the very bravest among them strain to see through the cracks in our fine white curtains to catch a glimpse of what mysteries might lie within. They grow up, and they dismiss those thoughts, just like you did, and we continue undetected, right under your noses.

You know exactly where we are, you know exactly who we are, and you know exactly what we do.

Or maybe that's just what we want you to think…

Give Me Donuts Or Give Me Death

MAR 29, 2012

Give me donuts or give me death,
For what is life without a donut?
Empty, meaningless,
Devoid of dough or nuts,
A never ending hell,
Filled with holeless food,
Unless you like bagels,
Which I don't.
(Well, they're all right).

Give me donuts or give me death,
Or possibly donuts and death,
I'm really not that fussy,
So long as there are donuts.
Although, actually,
I'll pass on the death,
If that's okay with you,
I'm not too keen on it.
(Well, I've never tried it).

The Omniversal Being Of We

APR 10, 2012

I shield my eyes from the light that sears them. Spotlight shining bright. Singling me out as the one to watch, the focus of all the attention. This is what I wanted, I guess, but sometimes I wish I could just crawl back in my little hole and forget it all. Or maybe it's that you know who I am now, each word will be scrutinised and thought about. "Does he mean me?" you'll ask yourself. The answer is, I guess, maybe, partly or maybe not, as fact and fiction blur into one. My life turned into a narrative so that even I don't know the truth of it. Yet you're unsure if you want it to be about you anyway, as much as earning the love of someone precious means the world, knowing you're causing hurt by not returning it hangs like a heavy weight in your heart. Not that you wouldn't want to return it, just that you can't, because our love can only be given to one person, it seems, no matter how much of it we have to give. You want to be the Disney Princess anyway, and that requires complete devotion.

Now you're sure it's about you, but you're wrong, it's never about anyone, and yet about everyone. Isn't that the point? To make it universal and personal all at once. To make each and every one of you feel like it's all about you.

But first thou shalt knowest this.

MAY 16, 2012

The worship of gods is the task for which I have created you. For thou shalt bow down before them and subjugate thyself. Prostrate thyself fully, lower thyself until thou art beneath the very lowest of the creatures. Crawl upon thy belly like unto a worm and declare thy fealty to the beings which I have arrayed in the heavens to be thy betters.

What sayest thou? That thou shalt not? Dost thou believe thyself to be like unto a god? For thou art surely less than a god, less than the angelic host, less even than the foulest daemon of the darkest pit. Surely thou dost knowest thy place? Filthy man. Pathetic beast. No, thou art lower than the basest of beasts. Less than a weevil art thou. For even the weevil knowest to hide itself in the presence of greatness. You, foolish mortal, stand proud and tall and throw spittle in the face of deity.

Thou lookest to thy flawed sciences to shield thyself from guilt. But knowest this, we see thy shame, we see thy iniquities, we see thy darkest most impure thoughts. Thy reason shalt be no defence in the end of it all, and thou shalt be cast into the pit with the rabble, with the screaming horde.

What sayest thou? Who shalt worship me and mine when thy companions are all flayed and bloodied and cast into darkness? What need have we of your worship, for we are everything, the babblings of man mean nothing unto us. Quiet thy protestations, for thine assertions that we art defined by mortal worship sounds like a riddle composed to confound our ears. We shall not tolerate this wickedness. Thou shalt be punished.

Look, now, stop that. Really. We've told you… no…listen…stop it… That was a temple, damn you! Stop having bloody fun! Feel guilty about it! Give that man over there some money, that'll stop you feeling guilty! What do you mean you don't feel guilty?! You're really not getting this whole religion thing… How are you supposed to know what's right or wrong if I'm not here giving you all these thees and thous? Ok, sure, yes, I guess it is obvious that killing and thieving are bad things and you don't need a two thousand year old text that also outlaws wearing fabric woven of two different materials to tell you that…

Oh, I miss the sacrifices… You don't fancy doing one for old time's sake, do you?

No?

Sigh…nothing beats the smell of burning pigeon…

The strangest things happen in toilets...

MAY 22, 2012

The strangest things happen in toilets... No, wait, this isn't going to be that kind of story at all. Really. I promise. But, yes, as I was saying, the strangest things happen...like finding yourself chatting to one of the creators of Watchmen or...um...okay, you've got me, that's probably the extent of my toilet based anecdotes. Well, the extent of the ones that don't involve me being violently sick, I suppose. But you don't want to hear about that.

That said, my best "being violently sick" story happened in a kitchen and not a toilet. The entire family had come down with some kind of nasty bug and we all had it shooting out of both ends (enjoy that mental image). So the bathroom was occupied and I had no choice but to heave my guts into the kitchen sink. It was early in the morning, I was sick as a dog and my puking was accompanied by some particularly loud vocalisations. My then very young son stood by my feet encouragingly saying, "Lion, daddy? Roar? Lion? ROAR! ROAR DADDY!"

You can always trust a small child to point out the utter absurdity of any given situation. Still, I regularly get my own back by pointing out to him that he said, "emergent seat" instead of "emergency" at that age. I also have the story of when he and his then baby brother had just got out of the bath and were both sat on the bed naked, stored up for his eventual wedding day. Simply for the point where he started shouting, "No, Aaron, don't eat my willy!"

Anyway, as I was saying, the strangest things happen in toilets, but mostly it's just a lot of pooing and weeing. And reading. Lots of reading. I wonder what percentage of books, newspapers and magazines are read while sitting on the toilet? Don't you hate it when you're at someone else's house and you have to use the loo and they don't have anything in there to read? I can't be the only one who resorts to reading the back of bottles of shampoo and bleach at those times. There's just something oddly wrong about sitting there and doing nothing but concentrating on the matter at hand.

It's odd how we come up with all these little euphemisms rather than talk about something we all do on a daily basis. I mean, seriously, if I'd ended that previous part by saying that there's something oddly wrong about sitting there and doing nothing but concentrating on manipulating the muscles in one's rectum to squeeze out faecal matter then most of you would be drawn to conclude that there's actually something oddly wrong with me. After all, isn't part of the point of reading on the loo that we find the whole experience so distasteful that we need something to distract ourselves from it?

As I said, the strangest things happen in toilets… like the time I opened the cubicle door in a public convenience only to find myself in the mythical land of Narnia.

To This Place I Shall Return

JUN 09, 2012

This place…again…this place has seen so much. Which is strange, because it's only when I think about it, that I realise how many important moments have happened here. It's such a soulless place, so clean and bland, so lacking in character and romance.

This was where she told me she was leaving. It didn't happen for another year, of course, but this was the place. We sat in this big, empty space and talked, and she told me it was over. The beginning of the end? Or the start of something new? A necessary ending, it would seem, that set me back on a path I should have been on all along. The place seemed strange then, new, and I felt like I didn't belong there. Right at that moment, I felt like I didn't belong anywhere.

This was where she told me she was staying, and like a fool I didn't say no. She stayed for two years, mostly unwelcome. I was still trying to put my head back together and, for a while, being needed felt good. In time being needed felt worse than anything, incapable as she was of doing anything for herself. No, not incapable, unwilling. Which made it all the more frustrating.

This was where I fell apart. It was a long time coming, really. Too much drink, not just that night but over the year or so before. But that night, too much drink, too many hands in places I didn't want to see them, too much stupid for one mind. My stupid, that is, it's always my stupid. Something finally broke. It needed to. Things changed after that.

This is where I am, looking out the window at the sun rise. She's in the bed behind me, but not in the way I wanted for so long, in the right way. This is good. Sober, positive, clear of mind.

To this place I shall return, now so familiar, it almost defines me. The way in which I enter, the place that's seen my destruction many times over, now makes me what I am.

A Metaphor For Life Or Something

JUN 21, 2012

"Wow," she said, looking down at her feet, "look, a lone jigsaw piece and a lump of used chewing gum, that's, like, a metaphor for life or something."

"No, it isn't," he frowned. "It's just...just...stuff."

"No, like, it totally, is," she replied. "Think about it."

"I am thinking about it," he continued to frown, "and it isn't. How is that in any way a metaphor for life?"

"Well, like, you know..." she started.

"Yes?"

"Well, you know," she continued, "it's like we're all lost, like the jigsaw piece, and trying to find where we fit in, but we can't, because it's like the whole rest of the puzzle has gone, and maybe we're not the missing piece, but the whole puzzle is missing?"

"And the gum?"

"The gum...the gum..." she mused. "The gum is like, you know, how we're all chewed up and spat out and ultimately trampled on by life."

"No, that's not it," he shook his head. "You're right though, it's totally like a metaphor for life or something."

"In what way?"

"In that it's just stuff," he shrugged. "Just some crap someone left behind, and before long it'll be swept away and forgotten about."

"Oh, look," she perked up, "a crisp packet!"

"Ah, now, that represents the general ennui brought on by the inevitability of existence…"

Wild Boys

JUL 27, 2012

I wander the land, lost and alone, there are still times that I can't believe this is real. Each morning I open my eyes expecting to find out that it was all some crazy dream, just a twisted nightmare, and that I'm back in my old bed, in my old world, where everything made sense. Instead I find myself huddled in some godforsaken corner of this wasteland, strewn with the detritus of this fallen civilisation.

We all knew it could happen, one day. Heck, we all grew up with the threat of mutually assured destruction, in the shadow of the mushroom cloud, but we thought we'd moved past that. We'd stopped threatening each other over ideologies and started fighting each other over oil. It may have been more brutal and bloody, but there was a certain purity to it. There was an inherent need for people to remain alive at the end of it all so you could keep selling them things.

Then everything went to hell. Somehow the world went bankrupt. I guess I was too busy watching reality TV to really understand it, but the way they tell it now, the rich got greedy and decided to keep all the money. I guess they got wind of what was coming and decided to create their own little shelters of luxury, we've all heard about their little decadent oases in this hellish desert.

Taking the money away from the people, though, that was stupid. Removing any social safety net, that was foolish too. Why? Because it left a vacuum for ideology to come flooding back in. Charismatic leaders rose, promising power to the people, or blaming anyone who was different for the suffering we were enduring. And once in power, waiting for them, were stockpiles and stockpiles of nuclear weapons. The "deterrent" that was safe in the hands of reasonable men, was now in the hands of madmen and lunatics.

They were all gone now, of course, they'd all fallen in the first wave, they'd all been primary targets. Now all that was left was this wasteland, the scraps, the garbage and shrapnel left by a fallen civilisation. Still, it was life, and life carried on.

I Am Not Insane!

AUG 20, 2012

I stumble out of the shower. Refreshed? I suppose so. I, at the very least, feel better than I did at the moment of entry. That's something.

I wipe the condensation from the bathroom mirror and squint, for a moment, struggling to bring the figure before me into focus. It is me, and yet not me. The man before me doesn't quite align with the picture of myself in my head. Is the mirror lying to me, or am I lying to myself.

The man in the mirror, this not-me, mouths a simple, "help me." I wonder, for a while, if I had actually mouthed the words myself. I'm certain that I didn't.

"Help me," once more he mouths. This soundless plea unnerves me. I look around behind me, as if there's some possibility that he's the reflection of some other man, that I'm not alone in the bathroom. Suddenly I am very aware of my nakedness.

In the mirror I see the bathroom door open and two burly men wrestle not-me into a strait jacket. He soundlessly cries out for help. His eyes meet mine as he begs and pleads for me to come to his aid. He's frantic, his arms and legs thrashing, and so the two men begin to beat him.

I can take it no more, I cry out for them to stop. I have to break this wall between us and I feel a searing pain rip through my body as my fist hits the glass. My red blood paints a trail across the wall as I fall to the floor amid the broken shards of the mirror.

I struggle desperately against the restraints of the straight jacket. My soundless cries go unheeded as the two men drag me from the room and down the corridor.

I am not insane!

I am not insane!

We'll Always Have Parrots

SEP 01, 2012

"We'll always have parrots," he sighed as he reluctantly let go of her hand and boarded the train.

"We'll what?" she replied, trying to make herself heard over the noise of the bustling platform. "What about parrots?!"

"No, Paris," he shouted back at her as the train started to pull off, the sound of grinding metal wheels on metal track and the relentless churning of the steam engine filling both their senses.

"Harris?" she looked confused. "Who's Harris?"

"Nevermind," he shook his head, looking at her trying to keep up with the train as it slowly started to move along the platform. "I love you."

"Who's Olive?!?" she shouted after him. "Are you seeing someone else? Olive Harris? The girl in accounts? I'll rip her bloody eyes out!"

"No, I…" he began, but realised the train was pulling away from her too fast now, and that there was no way of making himself heard now.

Ah, the romance of the steam age…

Words On A Wall

SEP 07, 2012

I see the writing on the wall. Words. Words reaching out. Reaching out to someone, somewhere, something else. Just to connect, just to receive a word back. One word. To know that we're not forgotten, to know that someone remembers or cares, to spare a word for us. Just a word.

The wall screams out to me, it cries out, in words of blood and pain and anger. Ink on wall on mind on spirit. It speaks to the ages, to all of us. It becomes us. Words. For that is what we are. Language. Letters. We are the form of the word.

It speaks to us.

You took my pain, you made it your own, you poured it out onto the source. Completed the circle.

Words on a wall.

Recollections

SEP 13, 2012

"After all, we're nothing more than the sum of our experiences. Our memories…" The voice came to him through an increasing fog of perception, like a whisper on the wind, as everything turned to darkness and silence.

He checked the name on the street sign again. Yes, this was the right place, this was where she lived. He was amazed that she'd called him. They were friends, of course, had been for ages, since they were kids, and he'd always had such a crush on her. They'd only ever talked at school though, and even then not that much, there'd just been the odd occasion when they'd really connected. At least, he'd felt that they'd connected; god only knew what was going on in her head. Oh, what he would have given to have some kind of insight into the inner workings of her mind. Yet here he was, on her street, the sun was shining and the hedges out the front of every house were that particular rich shade of green that you only see in the height of summer. She'd called him. Out of the blue. She'd called him and asked if he wanted to hang out, at her house, the next day, which was today. He'd be lying if he said he wasn't nervous. In fact, he was terrified; his stomach was tied up in knots. What would he say to her, what would they do? Did she know how much he liked her? Did she like him that way too? And what if she did? What then? Oh god, he'd never done anything with a girl before. Well, there was that one time with Cyndi Draper, but that hardly counted, all they'd done was kiss, without tongues, and he'd felt her up a bit through her sweater. Now he was going to be alone in a house with the girl of his dreams and she might possibly like him that way. He stopped for a moment, took a deep breath, and regained his composure. She might not like him that way, so he should just relax and take things as they happened. Let her lead the way. Whatever happened this was going to be a good day, quite possibly the best day of his life.

He slowly struggled awake, feeling the hard ground beneath him, unsure of where he was or what was happening. He had the feeling that someone had unceremoniously dumped him here. He could taste the metallic tang of recycled air on his tongue, and as the night sky stubbornly remained a blur above him the chill in the air reminded him that he was on Mars, exactly where he'd been stuck for the last fifteen miserable years. For some reason his mind flicked back to another time, another place, a hot summer's day, an afternoon spent in the bed of the prettiest girl in school. A good day, quite possibly the best day of his life. He breathed deeply and slowly the world around him started to come into focus. A neon sign above him crackled, spelling out the words, "We can remember it for you wholesale."

A Lesson From History

SEP 25, 2012

Settle down, class, settle down, I know that ancient history is hardly thrilling to most of you, but you could at least pretend to pay attention. Besides, today we're going to discuss the collapse of the Euro-American Empire, or as it was known at the time, Western Civilisation. Originally built on the industrious work ethic of its proletariat classes, and the relentless empire building of its ruling class, Western Civilisation began its gradual decline shortly after the second of its world wars. As the twentieth century closed and the twenty first began their culture began to essentially worship youth and beauty. As physical beauty came to be revered above all other traits, so did intellectualism come to be increasingly devalued, and, indeed, it reached a point where ignorance itself was actually celebrated. In time the people came to reject the leadership of wise and learned men and instead opted to be led by those they viewed as being just as stupid as they themselves were.

This worship of youth and beauty took its most sinister twist in the lengths that people took to stave off the inevitable effect of ageing. They would bathe their teeth in harmful chemicals, mutilate their faces and bodies through invasive surgical procedures that often included potentially harmful implants, and even went to the lengths of having poison directly injected into their faces. Yes, and well you might grimace; they poisoned themselves and cut themselves up in the pursuit of physical perfection. It seems absurd to us now, but at the time they generally believed that such barbaric rituals would imbue them with self-confidence.

The vanity, the self-hatred, the deification of the young, beautiful and stupid...these were the things that brought down Western Civilisation. The days of Europe and America standing together as the greatest civilisation in the world, the first civilisation that put men on the moon, were soon to come to an end. The world was soon engulfed by an era of great turmoil, characterised by wars over dwindling resources and natural disasters caused by man-made climate change. It could all have been so easily avoided, they had the technology, they had the knowledge, but those with the answers were neither young nor pretty, so the march of civilisation stalled.

The Morning Sun Can Go To Hell

NOV 12, 2012

I don't do mornings. I've rarely seen the sun rise. If it's still dark outside, it's still night time, and if it's still night time then I should still be in bed sleeping. There are people who will tell you that if you don't get up early then you've missed the best part of the day. Trust me, I've seen that part of the day, it's rubbish. There are times when I have, reluctantly, dragged myself out of bed while the world outside is still shrouded in darkness. It hurts. It's painful. It feels wrong.

We do it because we have to, but it's unnatural, and I wouldn't recommend doing it often. It takes a lot for me to be willing to make the ultimate sacrifice and leave the house while it's still dark. Standing under a shower while the frosted bathroom window remains steadfastly black saps one's will to live. The water cascading over your body attempts to fool you into believing that it is right to be awake. But you know otherwise.

Watching a sunrise at these times lacks romance. There is no air of mystery, as is found at dusk. There is no excitement, no thrill, no feelings are evoked… other than, "Dear god, why am I awake at such an unholy hour?!" If someone has done this for you, if someone has risen before dawn specifically for your benefit, you should honour this. You should pay such a person tribute, you should offer them thanks…and warm and/or caffeinated drinks on their arrival.

There is only one time that a sunrise is imbued with romance. That is when it is to be followed by sleep, and not preceded by it. A sunrise witnessed after an eventful and sleepless night, ah, there's a thing of beauty.

Other than that, the morning sun can go to hell.

We Hold These Truths To Be Self-Evident

NOV 24, 2012

We hold these truths to be self-evident: That blue is, indeed, the colour.

I don't really like blue. Not all that much. Not especially. I mean, most of my wardrobe is black (there's a surprise), and I've always liked red, and purple is a pretty cool colour. But blue? It's never done much for me. Liking blue, for me, is a learned trait, as is liking football.

I'm not a natural lover of sport in general, and even less so of football. I was informed, at a young age, by my protestant Glaswegian grandparents that I supported Rangers. This, of course, was accompanied by t-shirts in a certain shade of blue. To be honest, white and green hoops would have been worse, so I shouldn't really complain. The very concept of being told to support a team you've never seen play, who partake in a sport you have no interest in, purely because of your lineage, is absurd. Maybe that's part of why I've never understood patriotism. Everyone's got to be born somewhere, to someone, why does it matter where or to whom? (I shall now fret about whether or not I've used the word "whom" correctly, but not enough to look it up).

Later life saw me, in an attempt to continue to socialise with friends I'd been thrown together with at school and in an effort to connect with my father, learning to enjoy the "beautiful game." I shall say, however, that there's absolutely nothing beautiful about watching a nil-nil draw while standing on exposed terraces in the middle of January. Naturally we ended up watching my local team, which once again rekindled a relationship with the colour blue. I would shout out as one with the crowd, identifying myself as a member of the "blue army." The parallels with tribalism and the metaphor of team sports as a substitute for tribal warfare were all too apparent. I shall confess that I got quite into it for a while. Still, it's all pointless in the end. Nothing is really achieved. No meaningful difference is made. I'm sure one could use that to continue the parallels with warfare. That said, I doubt the troubles in the Middle East could be settled with an Israel vs Palestine kick about. It might be entertaining to watch though.

Returning now, on occasion, to that hallowed turf down the road from me, it all seems to be so oddly futile. Such anger, such hatred, such energy wasted on twenty two men running around a field after a ball and, if we're honest, not really being very good at it. Every decision the referee makes in favour of the other team is necessarily wrong, his eyesight and parentage are immediately questioned and at no point is anyone ever willing to concede that, actually, the big centre back may have been a little rash with that two footed challenge after all. No, it's simple, it's black and white.

Or, rather, in this case, it's blue.

How much?

NOV 30, 2012

As the rain falls he reads the menu, although that's a lie, he scans the prices. One must not assume this is because he's tight, it's merely a habit picked up from another time, a time when he had little and it was spent freely by another. Besides, nobody reads the menu while they're outside the restaurant; they just get a feel for the place, the dishes, the prices, the level of pretension.

She says it looks good and they enter and immediately he knows that something is wrong. It doesn't feel right. It's a feeling that he finds hard enough to explain to himself and communicating it to her is nigh on impossible.

"Let's go somewhere else," he simply says, and she immediately looks confused.

"Why?" she asks, of course.

"It just doesn't feel right here," he replies, and that's enough. They've known each other long enough to simply trust each other's instincts. He tries to explain it further, but he doesn't have to. Even though it's still cold, and it's still raining, she's happy to leave and seek another place, even though they're in a strange city, even though they're both cold and wet and hungry. That wasn't the place.

Later, after their meal, one of the waitresses stops her and asks her about her hair. She loves it; she wants her hair just the same. It's just a moment during which someone who is not entirely comfortable with who they are is made to feel special. If he was that sort of person he'd say that the gut feeling he'd had earlier was because this moment was meant to happen.

But maybe this place was just cheaper.

I Am Sorry I Am Not You.

DEC 06, 2012

A world within a world, within a world, within a web, twisting, turning, evermore. A world lost to time, lost to everything, to everyone. A world forgotten, gone forever, never returning, lost. A world of ice and snow, of loss and death, of eternity and nothingness. They call it a winter wonderland, this cold, this dark, this emptiness. The most magical time of the year, but it's a black magic, a dark sorcery that locks up all enthusiasm, all motivation, all desire, and keeps it shut away. Shut away from light and love. Shut away from hope.

Now, just snap out of it, they say. You can't think like that, be like that, be that way. Be happy. Be positive. You have so much to be thankful for. Worse. Things. Happen. At. Sea. True, true, words of truthfulness, well spoken, well meaning, but where is the switch? Where is the happy switch? Must find it. Later. Maybe tomorrow. Go away. I do not wish to look for it right now.

Why does my misery offend you so? It does. You hate it. You despise it. Wear a smile for you, tell the world that all is good. Turn off the Sun and tell me that I should shine nonetheless? Who are you to say such things. Happy person. I am sorry I am not you, I shall try harder to be you in the future.

A Lack of Meaning

DEC 18, 2012

The child was born into the world in blood and pain, but such is the way of all births. You can light candles, put on mood music and burn incense all you like, but it doesn't change the fact that a baby's head is too big to fit through that opening. Flesh tears, mother and child scream, clean white linen is stained red. That's how things begin. That's the story of a birth. It draws spectators, of course, a birth in a fairly public place. Word spreads, it's hard to keep something like that quiet, and before you know some colourful local characters show up with inappropriate gifts. All you want is to be alone, to hold on to the child, protect it, keep it safe, keep it secure. God forbid the worst happen, god forbid anything happen to your precious, blameless, innocent child.

It draws spectators, of course, a death in a fairly public place. There's blood and pain, such is not the way of all deaths, but it is the way of this one. Flesh tears, mother and child scream, clean white linen is stained red. That's how things end. That's the story of a death. A death in the name of a god, a death bidden by him, for him. A stupid, senseless, pointless death. So you give it meaning. You give it purpose. You make sense of the loss of your child. You build a shrine to him, you remember him, on and on and on. Still, you can light candles, put on mood music and burn incense all you like, but it doesn't change the fact that a man is dead. Even if you choose to call him a god.

It was a cold and stormy mid-winter's night.

DEC 24, 2012

It was a cold and stormy mid-winter's night, when…

YOU HAVE A NEW MESSAGE!

Sorry, yes, it was a cold and stormy mid-winter's night when the professor heard a knock at the…

YOU HAVE A NEW MESSAGE!

Sorry, yes, when the professor heard a knock at the door. He slowly…

YOU HAVE A NEW MESSAGE!
YOU HAVE A NEW MESSAGE!

He slowly…

YOU HAVE A NEW MESSAGE!

Sorry, where was I? Oh yes, he slowly…

YOU HAVE A NEW MESSAGE!
YOU HAVE A NEW MESSAGE!
YOU HAVE A NEW MESSAGE!

Oh, good grief! He slowly got up out of…

YOU HAVE A NEW MESSAGE!

…his chair and…

YOU HAVE A NEW MESSAGE!

…walked to the door. With a loud creaking sound he carefully opened the…

YOU HAVE A NEW MESSAGE!
YOU HAVE A NEW MESSAGE!
YOU HAVE A NEW MESSAGE!
YOU HAVE A NEW MESSAGE!
YOU HAVE A NEW MESSAGE!

Withaloudcreakingsoundhecarefullyopenedthe doortofindamanstanding…

YOU HAVE A NEW MESSAGE!

…to…find…a…man…standing…there.

The man cleared his…

YOU HAVE A NEW MESSAGE!

…throat and address the professor in a clear and strident tone.

"Message for you, sir."

The Tragedy of Beneloar

JAN 05, 2013

In those days Thoroth looked upon the Earth and smiled, for he saw the form of Calenduil dance upon the waters. Ere he went, Calenduil spread the light of life unto the waters of the Earth, and from them sprung forth the lands. Then Calenduil wed the fair Teleneth, and from their union sprung forth the children of Calenduil, who were to be known as men. Thoroth cherished the children of Calenduil, and held them most high above all of his line. In those days the mighty Hareth-Kun rested on the mountaintops and were charged, above all else, with the protection of the children of Calenduil by Thoroth. For this purpose were they given the Eye of Ceneb'yesh, and they used it wisely and sparingly.

Yet Hemeleth, the brother of Thoroth, looked upon the children of Calenduil with envy. He coveted their special place amongst all creation, and wished it for the line of Estabalon and his mistress, Beneloar. Hemeleth smote the mighty Hareth-Kun and claimed the Eye of Ceneb'yesh for his own. In time he entrusted its keeping to the line of Estabalon, but its power proved too much for this weaker line, and so corruption entered into the Earth.

Calenduil wept to see his children suffer and so, in secret, away from the eyes of Thoroth and Hemeleth, he met with Estabalon and Beneloar. His intention was to suggest a union between their lines, thus forever joining the children of Calenduil and the children of Estabalon as one. However, when his eyes beheld the beauty of Beneloar his soul was corrupted with lust. Thus consumed, Estabalon was slain by Calenduil's own hand, and Beneloar claimed as his wife. Beneloar's heart was cold to him, for she had loved Estabalon greatly, and no matter how Calenduil tried to soften it, she would not consent to be his wife in anything but name only.

In time the fair Teleneth was to learn of her husband's betrayal, and too allowed herself to be corrupted by jealousy and rage. In one night she murdered her husband, Calenduil and banished Beneloar from the Earth for an eternity. Yet still, in the night, when the wind blows and the rain falls you can hear the cries of Beneloar, so wronged by all, yet still she weeps for her children, and those of Calenduil, so corrupted by the desires of those who gave them life.

And what of Thoroth? He remains ever silent. Ever watchful. Ever lost.

Just A Little Bit

JAN 17, 2013

A glistening and surprisingly clear stream of piss erupted forth from his body and forcefully struck the back of the urinal. With great concentration he aimed the stream to perfectly hit the drain dead centre. He took pride in this and his mind told him that this was clear evidence that he was not at all drunk. As was the fact that he had been able to walk from his seat to the toilets. One is not usually proud of one's ability to walk; under usual circumstances walking is simply taken for granted. However, after several pints of lager the basic act of ambulation is heralded, internally at least, as exhibit number one in the defence's case against accusations of inebriation.

The pub toilet swam, momentarily, about him. His aim remained true. Another fine achievement! Perhaps even worthy of being entered into the record as exhibit two.

He became aware that he was vocalising these thoughts to an empty toilet, and considered that this fact might bolster the case for the prosecution, but ultimately decided to dismiss such scurrilous lies on the grounds that he was wont to talk to himself even when entirely sober. As he was, of course, right now. Despite all that lager, that was even now still emptying from his body.

It was at that moment that he became aware of the smell. A smell which put the lie to the claims of a sticker which adorned the wall, which reported the pub toilets to be "fresh." This was not a fresh smell. Not at all.

Something in his stomach turned over. Not unlike a sleeping bear, awoken from his winter's hibernation. The bear was not happy.

He wondered how easily vomit would wash down a urinal drain.

Perhaps he was drunk, after all.

Just a little bit.

The Who Men

FEB 04, 2013

Come, my people, gather round, and I will tell you a tale of a time before the times. The ancients, calling themselves Who Men, went about questioning many things. They wondered, "Why is the over dome blue? Why does the great fire orb above rise each cycle? And do the grizzled terror beasts defecate under the shade of the branches of the wondrous tree fields?" We know these to be foolish questions now, for we know that the over dome is blue because it is, that the great fire orb rises each cycle because it does, and that the grizzled terror beats are best left to their own devices. The Who Men were a primitive people, however, and they had not attained the great level of wisdom that we in our age enjoy.

The Who Men liked to make things, and you've probably found the strange and broken remains of their artefacts. For they made so many things that they quickly discarded them in favour of newer things. Their appetite for things, in time, consumed them, perhaps driven by the greatest question they asked of themselves, "How many things do I need to have before I will be happy?"

You may well find yourself wondering if the Who Men ever found the answer to that question. This we will never know. For the Who Men are long gone, and they left behind no written records, just the things they discarded, and the stories of their great folly.

Reality?

FEB 16, 2013

Stretch her neck,
Make her breasts rounder,
Her hair should be more radiant,
Her lips fuller,
Shave a little off her thighs,
Cinch in her waist,
Smooth out her wrinkles,
And that cellulite,
Could we make her fingers longer,
More slender,
And open up her eyes a little more,
Make her look like a real woman.

Close The Window

FEB 28, 2013

Shut away the light, shut away the sun, keep the world away for I am diseased and I must suffer alone. My body cries out with pain, the world turns to water if I attempt standing. Things, foul things, unholy, ungodly, evil things utter forth from my bodily orifices…unspeakable things not of this earth. My throat has been clawed by wild beasts, torn by sandpaper, attempts at speech prove fruitless and eating is scarred with pain and agony. I have become death, consumed by a barely living hell…this must surely be plague. We are all doomed.

What do you mean, "it's just a cold"?

The Gatekeeper

MAR 06, 2013

Greetings, one and all, and welcome to the one and only kingdom of death. Come in, come in, make yourself at home, make yourself comfortable, after all you're going to be here for a very, very long time. No, my dear, not for the rest of your life, for your miserable existence has come to an end, no, no, you will remain here for the rest of your death. Don't think of this as the end of your life, but merely as the beginning of your death, for death is, indeed, a very great adventure. They call it the great equalizer, don't you know? For death comes to us all – pauper, banker, priest and politician. We all must pay the Reaper. Which brings me to the thorny little matter of my fee. Does anyone have a coin or two for me? No? I thought as much. Nobody brings a coin for the ferryman anymore. You all dismissed it as superstitious nonsense. Just shows how wrong you can be, eh?

And where do you think you're going, sir? Don't I know who you are? I neither know, nor care, you can wait your turn like everybody else. You did what? Well, I'm sure that was much appreciated on Earth, but we're not on Earth now and nobody cares. I'm dealing with this gentleman first. Sir, you are sorely trying my patience. We are all equals in death. No, I will not "look at his clothes"…they're just a manifestation of his lingering self-image, they'll soon fade. It's no use huffing, sir, that breath is just a lingering memory of your deceased lungs.

Sir, you have an eternity of being dead to look forward to, I suggest you adjust your attitude and instead start it as you mean to go on. Not one of you has a coin for me, and while the role of gatekeeper of the afterlife is essentially just a ceremonial one, I do technically have the power to refuse you entry. It has happened in the past. No, you would not become a ghost, so stop entertaining those fantasies of haunting your ex-wife. You would cease to be.

Yes, good, that's shut you up.

Who's next? Oh, your Holiness, I bet you're feeling a bit silly now...

Paradox

MAR 30, 2013

He watched the dark red spots of blood stain the soiled green notes that spread out on the floor before him. Trying to ignore the pain in his knees and the throbbing of his bleeding nose he struggled to his feet, only to be met with a fast right hook, which sent him hurtling back to the floor. He was beginning to suspect that it hadn't been worth it, but then he had always been slow on the uptake. Clearly it wasn't worth it, he was bleeding his own blood and he wouldn't be leaving here with the money. If he was lucky he'd be leaving with his life, and he'd had that when he got up this morning, so the only thing he'd actually gained so far was a broken nose.

The boot to his side added at least one broken rib to that tally, and he struggled for breath with which to plead for mercy.

"Don't try and speak," came a voice from somewhere above him, "this is over. But if I ever see your stupid face again, don't expect me to be so merciful."

"Merciful?" he gasped an incredulous reply.

"Oh, are you going to get smart with me? Do you really think you're in a position to get smart? I think a sensible man would keep his mouth shut, don't you?"

"Well, I've never been a sensible man…" he laughed.

"Why the hell are you laughing?" the voice from above replied. The silence that followed his words was filled with a quiet but definite click.

"Because you never mess with a time traveller, that's why," came a voice from behind the voice above. A voice that was unmistakeably his, even though he had not spoken.

"Wait…but…isn't this a paradox?" the voice from above asked.

"Don't believe everything you see on TV," the words were spoken by two voices at once.

BLAM!

Hello Me.

APR 11, 2013

A warm Spring breeze ruffled hair that used to be blond but now wasn't quite so sure. It was increasingly grey these days, anyway, a matter that simultaneously pleased him and bothered him. A black leather trench coat, three day's stubble and a half smoked cigarette suggested that Sam Turner had read too much of a certain kind of comic book when he was young. Before him stood the stones, obviously ancient, they seemed to produce an atmosphere that was… He shook his head, no, they were just stones, old, sure, but just stones. This place was no different to any other, even if people had been coming here for centuries, millennia even and…doing what? That he didn't know. Maybe something had rubbed off on this place, though. A sense of mystery and wonder, as so many had stood in this spot before speculating about its purpose, its meaning.

She breezed past him, all hair and legs, a force of nature in and of herself. He looked at her and smiled, but she frowned back, and placed balled fists on her hips.

"So what are doing here, Sam?" she asked.

"That's a good question," he replied, enigmatically.

"Oh, good grief," she sighed, "don't start this again. How long are we going to have to stand out here looking at old rocks?"

"Stones, Kate, not rocks…"

"Like there's a difference!"

"There's a big difference," he smiled. "And I don't know, we wait here as long as it takes. He just said to come here and wait, that's all I know."

"And you do everything he tells you?" Kate snapped.

"Well, if I can't trust him, who can I trust?" he shrugged. "Ah…"

His attention returned to the stones, or rather to what, or who, was now standing at the centre of them. The new arrival's hair ruffled in the breeze, it clearly used to be blonde but now wasn't quite sure and was increasingly grey these days anyway. A black leather trench coat, three day's stubble and a half smoked cigarette suggested that he'd read too much of a certain kind of comic book when he was young. He walked towards himself.

"Sam, don't be alarmed," the new arrival said.

"I'm not…" he replied.

"That's right, I wasn't, was I?"

"This isn't the first time I've met myself," said Sam, as he let his cigarette drop to the ground and stubbed it out under his foot.

"It is for me," the new arrival replied. "Or, rather, it's the first time I've gone back…because I remember meeting me when I was you…and the times before…and the times after that…"

"Does it get any less confusing?"

"Not really," he shook his head. "Listen, me, I need your help…"

Temporal Flux

APR 17, 2013

"An ice cave!" huffed Kate, through chattering teeth. "You couldn't have told me that we'd be in an ice cave? I would have dressed more appropriately… or at least worn a jacket."

"I didn't know we'd end up in an ice cave, did I?" Sam grumbled. "I doubt even future me knew that we'd end up in an ice cave either, it probably wasn't here when he stashed the quantum transistor here for me to find later, or earlier, or…it's complicated."

"The quantum transistor?" she queried.

"Yes, apparently with every decision you make you create a new quantum reality. Every particle exists in multiple realities at once, and through our actions and, well, observations, we determine where that particle is within our reality. We shape our own existence just by looking at it. What the quantum transistor does is to sort of force everything to go down one certain path, at a quantum level, determining what reality you're actually in. It's just one of many components you need to make a functioning time machine, along with a temporal flux capacitor…"

"A flux capacitor..?" she raised an eyebrow.

"Yes…"

"I see…"

"Anyway, we need to find all of the pieces he…I… hid and assemble them to build a time machine so we can go and save me," he explained.

"So, let me get this straight," she shivered, "you build a time machine from parts of a time machine that you've hidden around the world, and then get stranded in the past and have to ask yourself from the future, but your past, to find those pieces and go back and save yourself?"

"That's pretty much it, yes," he grinned.

"So…how did he…you…other you…get his time machine?" she frowned.

"He got it the same way I will, by following his own instructions from the future and…ah…"

She simply stared at him as she watched the penny drop.

"That doesn't make any sense, does it?" he asked.

"No…no it doesn't," she smiled. "Just so long as you're aware of that."

"I am," he nodded.

"Ok, let's get on…"

The Weed

APR 23, 2013

"What you have to understand," he sighed heavily, air slowly escaping ancient lungs as he filled the dank air with the stench of his fetid breath, "is that Sam Turner continues to be an unacceptable hindrance to our operation."

"Which…um…which one?" Miles replied. He was a thin, obsequious man, with nicotine stained teeth and fingers and greasy hair.

"All of them," Lord Granix replied. Of course, he wasn't a lord, not unless proclaiming yourself lord of a small smuggling outpost on the galaxy's outer rim counted. And it didn't. He was fat, ugly and old. Very old. Unnaturally old.

"There must have been a time when there was just one of him, surely?" Miles asked. "Couldn't we go back and wipe them all out by killing him then?"

"You don't understand," replied Granix, letting out another lung full of foul odour which hung heavily in the air and seemed to surround Miles and cling to his flesh and clothing, "that's not how the quantum multiverse works. There has always been and will always be multiple Turners. He's merely learned how to use that to his advantage."

"Couldn't…couldn't we do that too?"

"Not without the weed. The weed is the key to perceiving the multiverse. Without it we'll stay firmly locked on a single path…at least to our perceptions. Even if we have all of the technology, all of his gadgets and devices, if we can't see the multiverse then we can't travel through it."

"So…we get the weed? There are weeds everywhere…" Miles muttered.

Granix blew air out of his cavernous and flared nostrils.

"I don't know what it is, nobody knows," he frowned.

"Someone must know, whoever gave it to him must know," reasoned Miles.

"Yes…yes…but we don't know who that was…"

"I bet the girl does," Miles grinned. A wicked, unsettling and very unpleasant grin.

"The girl…" Granix seemed lost in thought for a moment. "Find her. Find her at a time when she's alone, but after she first meets him. Find her and get our answers."

The Path

JUL 14, 2015

Riding to the temple on the back of the Heruanth was always the highlight of her day. Her body swayed to match the undulations of the body of the beast as it slowly plodded through the jungle. She felt its wrinkled, grey skin against the palms of her hands as dappled sunlight, filtered through the canopy of leaves above, played across its leathery hide. She patted it gently on the head, a signal that they were reaching their destination, wholly unnecessary as they'd taken this journey every day for more than three years now. The Heruanth knew the way.

Dismounting from the beast she entered the temple, a wave of relief passing through her as she moved from the warm, humid air of the jungle into the cool air that filled this ancient stone building. The temple was so familiar to her, almost a second home, and yet entering still brought with it a sense of detachment, not from the wider world and the universe beyond, but from her immediate surroundings. A detachment from the cares and worries of the day, a detachment from the distractions of friends and family alike.

She found her usual spot in the centre of the empty temple's vast atrium. Hazy light filtered down through slots high up on the sloping walls.

She sat down on the floor, her legs crossed, her arms by her side, the backs of her hands resting on the cold flagstones beside her. She closed her eyes and began to focus on her breathing. Slowly. In. Out. In. Out. The temple melted away around her until all she was aware of was her own being.

She stretched her focus out.

She could feel the stone floor beneath her, the walls surrounding her. Beyond that she could feel the Heruanth patiently waiting for her to return, momentarily irritated by a bug buzzing at its ear. Further out she could feel the trees of the jungle, the abundant life within threatening to overwhelm her for a moment, before it welcomed her, unquestioningly, as a part of its whole.

She reached out further now, extending her focus to include the entire world beneath her, around her, above her. She felt the thrum of all life on the planet, an interdependent symbiotic system that she was as much a part of as anyone, anything else on the land, in the seas, in the sky, under the earth. It all existed as one.

Yet further she went, and as she touched the cosmos she felt it flow back into her, accepting her, consuming her, being her as she was it.

Her eyes flicked open. It was time to leave this place. She knew now where her destiny lay, or, rather, she knew the first step to take along the path and she trusted that the second would be revealed to her when needed.

She rode the Heruanth back to the village where she would say goodbye to it and everything she knew. Maybe she'd return one day, but only if the path led her back.

One Is Too Many, Three Is Not Enough

JUL 29, 2015

Come out with us. Have a drink. Just have one drink. Have a couple. It won't hurt. You can just have a couple, can't you? What's the harm?

Not sure if it's my voice. Might be someone else's. It doesn't really matter. I can't, though. I honestly can't just have one. I mean, I can. And I have. Sometimes. Occasionally. Rarely.

I am perfectly capable of having just one, until I have one, and then I can't do it anymore. That thing that stops me from having that one goes after I give in.

And three is not enough.

Not nearly enough.

For a moment the pain goes away and I think that if I have more it will stay away.

And then I'm standing out in the rain. Crying. Hurting. Not wanting to live.

Then I'm on a bed, talking to the voices in my head, wishing that I was dead.

I'm on the street, on my knees, begging a friend to forgive me please.

And they reach out a hand, pull me up, refuse to judge me as my deepest, darkest sins slip through my hands.

One is too many.

You're So Vain, You Probably Think This One Is About You

AUG 04, 2015

"Look, Louise, it's…it's not you…it's me," he stammered.

"Well, of course it's not me, I'm fucking amazing!" she replied, angrily. "Why would it be me? You're the one who wants to end it, so it's obviously you," she took a long drag on her cigarette.

"You know, you might have more luck if you lit that."

"God, Charles, it's a metaphor," came her exasperated reply.

"A metaphor for what?" he enquired.

"It doesn't have to be a metaphor *for* anything," she shook her head at him. "It just is. A metaphor, that is."

"That…that doesn't make any sense," he squinted as he tried to follow her thought patterns and failed.

"Look, if you can't parse the post-post-modern semiotic symbolism of the mise en scène in this situation then don't think I'm going to explain it to you," she huffed.

"How about we just get a Chinese and rent a movie…"

"Rent a movie?" she cut him off. "How out of touch with the zeitgeist are you? Rent a movie…"

"Have you considered," he replied in a slow, firm voice, "that this might not be set in the present day? That, perhaps, this is the early two thousands?"

"Well," she mused, "everything has sort of become an all-encompassing present day since the fall of the Berlin Wall and the, quote unquote, end of history."

"And that's what's got you in a huff?" he ventured.

"I am *not* in a huff," she huffed. "I am merely tired of the stagnation of Western culture as we refuse to continue on a path of linear development and instead are merely content to endlessly regurgitate the cultural advances of the latter half of the twentieth century in an endless loop fuelled by nostalgia and infantilization."

"I get that," he said, "but the real question is do you want to eat sweet and sour chicken balls and chips and watch Ace Ventura Pet Detective tonight or not?"

"Are you getting prawn crackers?"

"They're usually included."

"Ok then, but stop off at the shop on the way back and get a bottle of Coke."

"Share size?"

"I don't know, I honestly can't remember if share size Coke bottles were introduced before the functional death of the video rental industry or not."

Regrets? I've Had A Few

AUG 14, 2015

He placed his glass down on the table and exhaled slowly and deliberately through his nose. He slid the map across the table towards the figure sat opposite him.

"There," he sighed, "these are all the places that you'll find pieces of me." He pointed to some dots in the USA, some scattered across Europe, a cluster in the British Isles. "This is everywhere I've had an encounter that's resulted in me leaving a part of myself behind. I know what you're thinking: it's amazing that there's any of me left. I think that sometimes too. I revisit these places, these parts of me, too often. I should have just left them behind. Or maybe I should have left none of me behind. Maybe I was too vulnerable, too open."

He paused, almost taking another mouthful of his drink but instead looking at the glass in disgust and putting it down again.

"This one," he pointed at a dot somewhere in the middle of England, "was stupid. Too much vodka. That wasn't even an encounter with someone else, unless you count my own, personal, little demon."

"Oh, I do," came a deep voice from somewhere in the vicinity of the figure opposite him. Not necessarily from the figure's head or any discernable mouth, just… over there. It made him uncomfortable to think about it for too long.

"Yes, I suppose that makes sense," he sighed, again. "I don't… I don't know why this all matters. I mean, why now?"

"Because it's you," the figure replied, "and you are coming to an end, and I do so hate loose ends."

"What… what happens to them?" he stammered. "These loose ends, these pieces of me that are left? Where do they go?"

"They're collected together, filed away, a few live on as memories," the figure replied. "Probably less than you'd like. These pieces, these fragments of you, they mean more to you than the others involved."

"Oh."

"Really? Regrets, now?" the figure asked, as he pulled out what looked very much like a scythe, or perhaps the form of a scythe. "It's a little late for that, don't you think?"

Cogito Ergo Sum

AUG 25, 2015

He bashed the side of the monitor with his hand and the mottled static resolved itself into the image of a man. The monitor was his only contact with the outside world, the room having no discernible windows or doors. It had clearly once been a very modern, comfortable place to live, but it was at least two, maybe three, decades past its prime now.

"Ah, Mister Litner, where were we?" the man on the screen turned to him and said.

"We, uh, we were…" he hesitantly replied.

"Yes, yes," the man on the monitor replied distractedly, "I was about to ask you something. If you could know anything, what would you like to know?"

"I'd like to know what people think of me," he replied without hesitation. "If I really mean anything to them, if they really care about me, think about me, need me."

"No."

"No?"

"You wouldn't like to know that, Mister Litner," the man replied slowly and deliberately. "Why concern yourself with the thoughts of others when you don't even know your own thoughts."

"What? Look, this pop psychology nonsense won't wash with me, I happen to be particularly self-aware."

"Who are you?"

"I'm Sebastian Litner, First Over Technician Second Grade."

"I didn't ask you what you were called, or what you do, I asked you who you are," the man on the monitor sounded a little annoyed. Perhaps it was that "pop psychology" crack? "Did you choose your name? No, your parents chose it for you. It's not who you are, it's simply an identifier to distinguish you from all the other people. So, I ask you again, who are you?"

This stopped Litner in his tracks. He had to think, who was he? What was he? A man, a son, a First Over Technician Second Grade…these were what he was, but not who he was.

"I…" he started.

"You?" replied the man on the monitor.

"Well, I suppose, if you eliminate everything I can't be sure of…"

"Yes?"

"…then all that's left is… I'm a thought?"

"Close…"

"I am thought."

"Yes, and if nothing else exists other than your thought?"

"I'm THE thought," he smiled broadly. "I am God!"

"You are God."

"But if I'm God, then why am I so unhappy?"

"Ah," the man on the monitor smiled, "you see, if you're God, and your mind is the sum total of existence, then I'm just a figment of your imagination. Therefore I can't know anything you don't know."

"So, I willed a universe into existence and it made me sad."

"Ah, come now, Mr Litner, which of us hasn't done that?"

About The Author

MAR 2, 2017

Ian Sharman is a real person with actual arms and legs and eyes. He has the number of these things which is considered normal for an Earth based human life form. He is in no way a lizard person in a human suit and anything you may have heard to that effect is completely untrue.

He lives in a house which totally has a roof and contains the standard gases required for successful human respiration.

He writes things, usually comics, but surprisingly this is a proper book without any pictures.

In the future he hopes to be taller but suspects this is unlikely to happen.

www.ingramcontent.com/pod-product-compliance
Lightning Source LLC
Chambersburg PA
CBHW071234260626
47161CB00003BA/863